OTHE
JEAN PAMFILOFF

MW01133796

COMING SOON!
The Goddess of Forgetfulness (Book 4, Immortal Matchmakers, Inc. Series)
Skinny Pants (Book 3, The Happy Pants Café Series)
Check (Part 3, Mr. Rook's Island Series)
Digging A Hole (Book 3, The Ohellno Series)

THE ACCIDENTALLY YOURS SERIES
(Paranormal Romance/Humor)
Accidentally in Love with…a God? (Book 1)
Accidentally Married to…a Vampire? (Book 2)
Sun God Seeks…Surrogate? (Book 3)
Accidentally…Evil? (a Novella) (Book 3.5)
Vampires Need Not…Apply? (Book 4)
Accidentally…Cimil? (a Novella) (Book 4.5) ← You are here. ☺
Accidentally…Over? (Series Finale) (Book 5)

THE FATE BOOK SERIES
(Standalones/New Adult Suspense/Humor)
Fate Book
Fate Book Two

THE FUGLY SERIES
(Standalones/Contemporary Romance)
fugly
it's a fugly life

THE HAPPY PANTS SERIES
(Standalones/Romantic Comedy)
The Happy Pants Café (Prequel)
Tailored for Trouble (Book 1)
Leather Pants (Book 2)
Skinny Pants (Book 3) SPRING 2018

IMMORTAL MATCHMAKERS, INC., SERIES
(Standalones/Paranormal/Humor)
The Immortal Matchmakers (Book 1)
Tommaso (Book 2)
God of Wine (Book 3)
The Goddess of Forgetfulness (Book 4) WINTER 2017

THE KING SERIES
(Dark Fantasy)
King's (Book 1)
King for a Day (Book 2)
King of Me (Book 3)
Mack (Book 4)
Ten Club (Series Finale, Book 5)

THE MERMEN TRILOGY
(Dark Fantasy)
Mermen (Book 1)
MerMadmen (Book 2)
MerCiless (Book 3)

MR. ROOK'S ISLAND SERIES
(Romantic Suspense)
Mr. Rook (Part 1)
Pawn (Part 2)
Check (Part 3) COMING 2018

THE OHELLNO SERIES
(Standalones/New Adult/Romantic Comedy)
Smart Tass (Book 1)
Oh Henry (Book 2)
Digging A Hole (Book 3) COMING 2018

Accidentally... Cimil?

An Accidentally Yours Novella

BOOK 4.5 OF THE ACCIDENTALLY YOURS SERIES

MIMI JEAN PAMFILOFF

A Mimi Boutique Novel

Cover Design by Earthly Charms (www.earthlycharms.com)
Creative Editing by Latoya C. Smith (lcsliterary.com)
Proof Reading by Pauline Nolet (www.paulinenolet.com)
Formatting by bbebooksthailand.com

Like "Free" Pirated Books?
Then Ask Yourself This Question: WHO ARE THESE PEOPLE I'M HELPING?

What sort of person or organization would put up a website that uses stolen work (or encourages its users to share stolen work) in order to make money for themselves, either through website traffic or direct sales?

Haven't you ever wondered?

Putting up thousands of pirated books onto a website or creating those anonymous ebook file sharing sites takes time and resources. Quite a lot, actually.

So who are these people? Do you think they're decent, ethical people with good intentions? Why do they set up camp anonymously in countries where they can't easily be touched? And the money they make from advertising every time you go to their website, or through selling stolen work, **what are they using if for?**

The answer is you don't know.

They could be terrorists, organized criminals, or just greedy bastards. But one thing we DO know is that

THEY ARE CRIMINALS who don't care about you, your family, or me and mine.

And their intentions can't be good.

And every time you illegally share or download a book, YOU ARE HELPING these people. Meanwhile, people like me, who work to support a family and children, are left wondering why anyone would condone this.

So please, please ask yourself who YOU are HELPING when you support ebook piracy and then ask yourself who you are HURTING.

And for those who legally purchased/borrowed/ obtained my work from a reputable retailer (not sure, just ask me!) muchas thank yous! You rock.

Dedicated to my awesome fans.
For the hysterical, and I mean hysterical, conversations
about very strange deities and also for your
contributions to the fake Cimil lines.

ACCIDENTALLY ...CIMIL?

Spot the Phony Cimil Line

Which one of these lines was *not* said by Cimil?

1. "Welcome to my insane world. Please keep your hands inside the unicorn at all times."
2. "Berty, you think you're badass with that outfit? Your tiny manly parts will be on display when I dump you on the floor."
3. "Shit is my middle name. Except on Wednesdays when I speak Klingon, then it's Baktag."
4. "F***ing Cub Scouts. Give them some mistletoe and a few Christmas carols and they think they own the whole f***ing holiday!"
5. "Roberrrrrto, that man-skirt is not bringing sexy back."
6. "Okay, I am a good goddess. I am a kind goddess, oh, hell. No, I'm not."
7. "Oh! Pluck, Pluck, Eyeball is my favorite game! It's like Duck, Duck, Goose…but with eyeballs!"
8. "Helpful is my middle name—except on Saturdays. Then it's Jaaaasmine…"
9. "Roberto, baby, how many times do I have to tell you? You're MUCH bigger than my unicorn!"
10. "You may be the big-shot Pharaoh Narmer now, but you're still not wearing my pretty pink skirt to the pyramid celebration no matter how well it swirls when you shift."
11. "Hey, Roberto, baby, starting the goth craze early with all that eyeliner."

SEE ANSWERS IN BACK.

WARNING:

SHORT STORY ahead! This novella will leave you hanging in suspense and may trigger frothing at the mouth and an urge to send the writer hate mail until the release of the series finale, Book #5, *ACCIDENTALLY...OVER?*

Enjoy, everyone!

Prologue

After all he has done to me, I still find myself unable to fully blame him. Because truthfully, some women aren't meant to be loved. And by some women, I mean me.

I. Am. Evil.

The *worst* kind of evil.

There are no limits to the death, destruction, and mayhem I will bring to your doorstep if it suits my needs. I will pretend to be your ally. I will pretend to give a rat's ass about your happiness when in reality only one thing matters. Survival. Okay, survival and avoiding naked clowns.

Judge me if you will, but this is the cold, hard truth about being the Goddess of the Underworld. Because I've seen the future. It holds no joy or hope. There is no sunlight. No love. No glorious garage sales where once useful items are given a second chance at a new life. There is only death. So much death.

And it's up to me to stop it. Me alone.

Okay, Minky and me, but mostly me. Potatoes, patatoes.

And what's my plan? Try to forget *him*. And

avoid watching *Love Boat* marathons. And definitely avoid bugs. Can't afford any distractions. Not now. Not when this giant mess is all my fault.

Why did I ever dare to dream that I could find love and happiness?

I. Am. Evil.

Or maybe I'm just crazy…

PART ONE—
CIMIL AND NARMER
THE EARLY YEARS

Chapter One

3000 BC (Give or take a few centuries. Who the hell's counting?)

The day started like any other. A typical day in the life of a goddess. An ancient, lonely, bored-out-of-her-immortal-skull goddess.

I opened my mind to my brethren, listened to their thoughts (*yawn*), felt their worries (*trivial*), and contemplated my otherworldly navel until I decided where my talents were most needed in the world. On this day, that meant checking in on my brother Kinich, God of the Sun, whose self-imposed exile was seriously getting on everyone's last nerve.

Especially mine.

Don't get me wrong; I was also worried. What affected him affected all of us. We were connected. Brethren of the same light. And we all tasted his pain, which was why I could say... *What a big baby!*

Yes, yes, it sucked to be a deity, a slave to mankind's well-being with no end in sight, no hope of finding true love, owning a pet sea turtle (don't ask), or of having a life, but that was the gig. How many millennia did it take to sink in? Apparently, for

Kinich, more than two. Or three. Or four. It was time to bring him back to our realm, time to take his place among us.

So I hopped into the portal, which spat me out in the usual place—a cenote in Mexico (See definition in back. Okay? Did you do it? Did you? Good. And moving on…)—summoned Minky my trusty unicorn; longingly stroked a sea turtle; and dashed off to Giza, Egypt, where Kinich was hiding out. Like I said, a typical day.

Jealous? Well, don't be. I haven't gotten to the real story yet.

Cue jazz hands and waffly waves of air for extended flashback…

It all started when I arrived at the small dusty market. Normally, this section of Giza bustled with camels, caged birds, and those other stinky animals—humans—but on this particular day, the place was a ghost town. When I asked Minky to do a quick sweep of the city, she immediately reported back. The masses were gathered outside the pharaoh's palace for a big speech. Naturally, we went to check it out, and that was when I saw *him*.

Hello, man candy!

As I stood at the foot of his great temple, the desert sun glistened off his rippling abs and deeply tanned bare chest, his golden staff gripped in his large, powerful hand (Yes, yes. I mean a real staff! Not his man-trinket. Jeez…). In typical pharaoh fashion, he had a razor-thin beard, more like a sculpted five o'clock shadow, along the very edge of his jaw and an elaborately braided goatee, which we shall call a pharaoh-tee. 'Cause this hottie was no goat. He was more of a huge frigging viper in a man's skin—deadly, powerful, with a barbaric gleam in his eyes. He wore a tall black-and-gold headdress that on any other man would scream "please kick my ass," but on him, it looked pharaoh-licious.

I licked my lips and watched with sheer fascination as his dark eyes drilled into the crowd, daring anyone to step forward and defy him. I shivered from the raw potency of his male strength. And when our eyes met for the briefest of moments, it felt like being hit with a bolt of lightning. Naughty, dirty lightning.

Who. Is. That? I thought. Yes, yes. I knew he was the king. But who was he really? What made him tick? Why did he glow with an intoxicating inner light that drew me in like a multifamily hut sale? (The BC version of a garage sale, but with pelts, used stoneware—yes, yes, made from real stone—and the occasional old donkey.) Point was, something about him was utterly irresistible. Why?

Inquiring immortal minds want to know...

Immortal minds also wanted to know what it would take to knock that pretty, pretty man off his pretty, pretty pedestal. I wanted to own him. I wanted to bend him to my will and have him begging me for attention. I wanted to *break* him.

Now, before you judge, my precious little people-pets, I'll refer you back to the earlier part of my story. The part where I tell you I am ancient, lonely, and bored. I can't help who I am or that when I see a mortal such as him, it feels like receiving a shiny new toy from the Universe herself.

And Auntie Cimi wants to play.

I elbowed the bald man to my side, standing with me among an ocean of loyal subjects who'd come to listen to their pharaoh publicly decree that from this day forward, Egypt would be a united people.

"Tell me," I said in the man's native tongue, "where does your king spend his nights?"

The man's shendyt—a simple pleated, white linen skirt—and golden armband told me he was a slave. One who belonged to the king, perhaps serving food or providing entertainment.

The human didn't answer, but instead stared nervously. I got that reaction a lot. Sometimes I wore my hair bobbed, sometimes long and wild, as it was today, but it was always flaming red and equally as uncommon as my pale skin and turquoise eyes.

Thank the gods that mortals can't see Minky. I gripped the slave's shoulder and stared deeply into his eyes. "Tell me your name."

The man blinked several times. "Adom."

Adom means "receives help from the gods." It's his lucky day!

"Adom," I said, "you will tell me everything you

know about your pharaoh, and in exchange, you will be free. Forever. You will be transported anywhere you like and given a purse of gold coins."

The man nodded slowly and pointed north.

I am a good goddess. I am a gentle goddess. I am a patient goddess. I will not turn him into a dung beetle. "You'll have to be more specific," I said.

"T-t-temple of the Sun. Temple of Ra."

Hmmm...how ironic. I'd actually come to Egypt looking for a real live sun god. Of course, Kinich didn't really hang out in temples, given he pretended to be a commoner. A seven-foot, golden-haired commoner with turquoise eyes. At least his tan fit right in.

"Is your king married? Got a girlfriend? What kind of music does he like? Ska revival? Dubstep? Oh, wait! I know, eighties love ballads!" I had to imagine a male as beautiful and strong as the pharaoh had hundreds of willing women at his beck and call. And what better music for a stud-gyptian like him than Journey?

Adom shook his head no. "I do not understand your words."

I sighed. That was my problem; no one did. Probably due to the fact that the dead constantly chattered away in the background of my mind—a sound reminiscent of a really, really big cocktail party—sharing every memory they'd ever had. They also existed in a place beyond the confines of time. They were from the future and the past, which made it extremely difficult to keep the present straight inside my head.

"Skip the music question, spanky. Just tell me about his love situation," I said.

"But I am named Adom, my lady."

"Oh, spanky, have you learned nothing yet?" I smiled sweetly. "Now speak! Or I'll rip off your toenails!"

"My king," Adom explained nervously, "has taken a vow of chastity until he finds his queen. He believes women rob men of their power and will only share his with her."

Oh. Now this just got a whole hell of a lot more interesting. Because if there was one thing I liked more than tasty, powerful mortals (and playing with them like a cat plays with a mouse), it was a challenge.

"So if he *were* on the prowl," I asked, "what flavor would he go for? Chocolate, strawberry, peanut butter banana?"

Adom stared blankly, a dribble of sweat streaming from his temple, his shiny brown head reflecting the hot desert sun.

Ugh. "What kind of women does he like?"

"I do not know. I have never seen him with a woman."

Dang it. Curse you, nature! You think you're sooo funny taking the cutest ones away from us girls!

I sighed. "Are you *sure* he would not like me? I come in all flavors of crazy. Most men, even those who prefer a hockey stick to a puck, want a little lick."

"I-I-I cannot say. You are very frightening."

True. So true. But...

"That's not what I meant. Oh, never mind! I will simply have to see for myself. Off with you!" I patted Adom on the head and looked up, up, up at Minky, who was about the size of my pet whale. Of course, Minky only had one head and was invisible. The moment my friend Adom touched her, he would be invisible, too.

"Minky, baby, go with Adom. Once you are out of sight, you know what to do." She'd take him anywhere he liked and give him as much gold as he could carry. I always kept a few hundred pounds strapped to Minky's saddle. One never knew when one might find a good sale. Or encounter a bribable sea turtle. (Don't ask.)

Minky flailed her head and neighed.

"Yes," I replied. "I'll be in the sun god suite when you return." I turned to Adom. "All righty! Off you go! See ya, papi." I gave Adom a pat on the tushy. "Fly! Be free!"

Adom zombied off through the crowd with Minky on his tail.

As for me? I had a sun god to hunt down before my date with a power-hungry, pious mortal who'd finally met his match.

Damn straight, women rob men of their power. Especially when it came to me.

Just after midnight, I approached the massive rectangular doorway of the temple of the sun. I'd spent the day combing dusty markets, smelling the stench of ripe animal dung, and asking around for Kinich. People knew who he was, but not where, which meant he was likely on another extended nude sunbathing excursion in the desert or off praying to the Creator to make him mortal. Who knew? I'd send Minky out to search when she returned. But point was, I really needed a little fun time to wash away my pissy mood. This part of the world was blistering, sandy, and the human males did not grant me a shred of cred when I told them I'd lop off their hands if they groped me.

For the record, it's seriously no fun lopping off men's hands when they don't see it coming. It's the screaming leading up to the lopping event that makes the punishment magical!

In any case, someone needed to teach these horny sycophants some manners—a topic I planned to bring up with Mr. Hunky Skirt after I hobbled his royal ego and wrapped him around my immortal pinkie. After I determined which ice cream he preferred, that was. Nut delight or soft-serve?

Cloaked in a black shroud, I approached the two bare-chested guards wearing manly microminis and then paused in front of the stone fire pit at the entrance. I gazed appreciatively at the torch-lit, glyph-covered walls. The structure itself was quite impressive. So monumental, in fact, that from a distance, the giant statues of Ra—the Egyptian sun god—to either side of the grand entryway appeared as tiny figurines balancing oranges atop their heads.

"Evenin' there, cowboys. What are your names?" I unveiled my head and watched the firelight dance in their pupils as they took me in.

"Where did she come from?" gasped the man on the left.

"She must be a creature from the bowels of the underworld," said the man on the right.

I shot Righty the stink eye before I stomped his toes with my sandal-clad foot. "Oh now, that was just rude. Do I *look* like I came from a bowel?" I opened my cloak and revealed my very skimpy white halter, busty chest, and little white sarong. I'd made both from panels of linen I'd "borrowed" from a merchant in the market. "Where's the chivalry? Really? I bet you don't get many dates, do you?"

The man trembled and blinked.

"Serenity, big boy. Serenity." I closed my cloak. "Actually, I am the Goddess of the Underworld. And by the way, I'm pretty tired of being mistaken for a man. Osiris? Oooh, please! Do I *look* like an Osiris?"

The two men stared blankly.

"Fine. Clearly we won't resolve this now. Take me to your leader," I said in a deep, ominous voice.

Suddenly, I spotted a beetle scuttling across the entryway, heading toward my foot. *Ewww!* I stomped on it, smashing the tiny villain into an unrecognizable pulp.

The two men gasped. "You killed a sacred scarab," said Righty.

I rolled my eyes. "I'm just getting started. Wait till you see what I do to your king. Now move it, princess!"

The man on the left lowered his spear and pointed it at my chest.

Grrrr…time for a little game of Cimi Says. I switched to my compelling voice and repeated my instructions. If that didn't get him moving fast enough, then I'd simply call upon one of my many other gifts. And let me tell you, I had hundreds of tricks up my proverbial sleeve. Far more than any of my brethren. Pain, compelling, bug makeovers, physical strength, the ability to sniff out a bargain, speaking all languages, speaking to the dead, nabbing souls, calligraphy, the list went on and on.

What was my secret?

Those Mexican cenotes (freshwater pools we used as portals, for you people who didn't listen to me and look up the word as I commanded) were jacked up with the most concentrated, supernatural energy known to god-kind, straight from the River of Tlaloc, which flows between our two dimensions, creating a fabulous superhighway for me and my thirteen brothers and sisters. Now, if you don't know my brethren, I'll fill you in later—they're quite the funky bunch—but the point I'm making is that the river has power. Learn to tap into it, and it's a deity Flintstone vitamin, and by deity, I mean me. I'm the only one who's figured it all out. That's why I am undefeatable.

"Right this way," said Lefty. I didn't know if he was a lefty, but he was the man on the left, so I christened him Lefty.

The two men led me inside, through a maze of lavishly adorned chambers, and then out to a large private garden. Statues and fire pits lined the stone walkway that led to the steps of a smaller temple, where two more guards stood with spears crossed over the doorway.

"She is here to see our pharaoh," said Righty.

The two new door jockeys exchanged glances. "No one enters."

Ugh. I don't have time for this. I pushed past Lefty and Righty. "Take me. Now." I commanded the two new plebes. They didn't move.

"What if I offer you a sandwich?" I winked provocatively.

They exchanged glances, clearly intrigued by my offer of this mysterious thing called a "sandwich," but didn't budge. Little did they know how males from the future would covet said sandwich. Almost as much as pizza, beer, and porn.

"Fine. Hardball it is! Move. Now," I said, using my compelling voice.

They pulled back their spears but then froze in place with awkward, uncomfortably contorted faces.

Darn it. I brain locked them. Sometimes it happened. Nobody ever said my powers were perfect.

"Everyone stay put until I return," I grumbled. "And don't let anyone in. I'm sure your pharaoh won't want to be bothered. Unless he's into nut delight, in which case, I'll be right back."

I left the four men behind and entered the temple. "Now, where the hell is my man cand—" My jaw dropped the moment I entered the spacious sleeping chamber and spotted the king standing outside on his private terrace, gazing up at the night sky, wearing nothing but a teeny-tiny, tight little man-skirt. No man-panty lines, either, which obviously meant he was one piece of cloth away from being perfect (aka naked).

Well, hellooooo, cowboy!

Twisted into tiny plaits adorned with gold beads and thread, his long black hair cascaded down the center of his deeply tanned, broad back. His smooth skin rippled with powerful muscles, two of which were his hard ass.

I sucked in an equally hard breath. That hard ass was connected to the most gorgeous set of powerful, manly thighs I'd ever seen on a mortal. I could only imagine what hung down the other side.

"Are you going to say something or simply stand there all night staring at my ass?" he said in a deep, calm voice, not bothering to turn around.

"Was that a trick question? Obviously, I'm going to stare at your ass."

From the moment the strange woman entered his chamber, he knew she was there. Her energy filled the room like a fragrant oil fills the nostrils.

Of course, he had been expecting her. A prayer to the Goddess Bastet never went unanswered when one's heart was true to the deities and of divine origin, as was his.

And when the woman arrived, he looked out across the dark, star-filled sky, thanking the deities for delivering his wish: a divine female worthy of his greatness, to worship his strength and power, and to provide him with many heirs to rule after his mortal shell crossed over the glorious banks of the Nile to join the gods for eternity.

"I've been expecting you." He turned, proudly showing off his cloaked but prominently displayed phallus. After all, there was no purpose in hiding his glorious erection. It was a badge of honor, a sign of his superior, kingly virility. And of his desperation to end the self-imposed sexual drought. He'd vowed to the gods to abstain until her arrival, confident they would be pleased by his sacrifice and deliver his request.

They had. Delivered, that was. There were simply a few unexpected turns. Nothing a powerful pharaoh could not handle.

What mattered was that his agony was finally over. He would bed her immediately, this very evening, and plant his seed. The ceremonies and public declarations to appease the subjects could come after he'd had his fill of her silky, pale thighs and saw the sure signs of a new life within her.

The woman's wide, jewel-colored eyes dropped to his shaft and drank him in without shame. "Is that a pyramid in your man-skirt, or are you hiding my unicorn?"

"You like what you see?" he asked.

"Does a sea turtle play hopscotch when no one's looking? Do naked clowns run in terror when they see me coming? Does Bigfoot have a 'Rides Free on Saturdays' pass for Minky?" She stared blankly and then sighed loudly. "Yes. The answer is…yes!"

What odd phrases this woman speaks. "Good. This pleases me. There will be no room for shyness in my bed." He reached for her chin, instantly feeling a powerful burst of energy course through him. He made a point not to react; he'd been expecting a goddess, after all. He tilted her head and stared down at her. "You are very small but quite lovely. I could not have picked better myself." *Yes, she will make a fine queen.*

He yanked off his shendyt and pointed toward the large sleeping platform covered with the finest pillows and softest sheets known to man. "Now disrobe and lie down so that I may enjoy the pleasures of your divine flesh."

Chapter Two

(Yep. Still in 3000 BC.)

Well. Not what I was expecting from the king. I felt my left eye tick with anger. Had this...*man*, this lowly mortal, commanded me to strip and get into his bed? Me?

And...is he really, really showing me his scepter? Don't get me wrong, I was more than pleased to learn I floated the pharaoh's felucca, but frankly, I expected more of a challenge. This guy was ready to show me his treasure, and all I had to do was walk through the door. What happened to his vow of celibacy? *Darn it. Easy men are no fun!*

I suppose it will be equally fun teaching him a bit of humility. Clearly he'd never had to work for a woman's affection. Clearly his sense of reality was grossly distorted by his gilded cage. Clearly he had no idea who he was dealing with: The most powerful deity in the universe. One who claimed souls just for kicks and spoke to the dead. I saw the future, the past, and the present through their eyes. I'd mastered the power of the River of Tlaloc! Dammit. I had a godsdamned unicorn! Yet he thought he could command me like a two-camel whore?

But did you see his beast-sized penis?

I shrugged. "Okay!" I shed my robe and hopped onto his bed.

He stared with a peculiar grin.

"What? You were expecting me to cower?" I patted the space to my side. "I'm waiting."

"Well, I—uhhh…" He tilted his head. "You are a very peculiar goddess. From where did you come?"

Good frigging question. "Where did *you* come from?"

He lifted his chin and crossed his arms over his brawny chest. "You are not in a position to ask questions of me, woman."

"I'm not?"

His eye twitched with anger. "That was another question."

"So is this. Ready? What's the difference between a hooker and a crack dealer?" Oh, he was so going to love this!

"My patience wears thin, woman. You will cease speaking in tongues and asking questions!"

"The hooker can wash her crack and sell it again!" I burst out laughing and rolled onto my stomach, using one of his pillows—*ooh, soft!*—to mop up the tears pouring from my face. Gods, I hadn't had this good of a chuckle for a few decades. *This feels fantastic.*

The pharaoh flipped me over. "You dare mock me? I do not care what you are, I will have you whipped if you do not curb your tongue, woman."

My chuckle died as I considered grabbing that giant penis of his and giving it a little twist and shout.

No, that would be unfair. His penis has done nothing wrong.

Yet. But one can certainly hope!

I stared into the depths of his pupils, the light of the small lamp flickering in his eyes. And that was when I saw it.

"Holy camel shit!" I scrambled away and jumped off the bed, placing my back against the stone wall. "What the hell?" I couldn't begin to articulate what I'd seen. Him, me, the birth of the Universe, the death of everything. Happiness. Destruction. Light. Darkness. All possibilities simultaneously existing on the tip of a needle. One point in time deciding everyone's fate.

"Who are you?" I blinked and stared at his deeply tanned face. His high cheekbones and full lips were exquisitely masculine, and his thick black brows only accentuated the man's natural ferocity.

He marched over, chest heaving with livid thoughts. "I am a king. *Your* king. Bow down before me and vow your loyalty." His giant bicep bulged as he pointed to the floor. "Bow!" he screamed.

For the first time in my existence, I didn't know what to do. My mind was a blank. A mortal—an arrogant, sexy mortal—had ordered me to grovel, and all I could think of was...

Nothing? No revenge. No lighting his hair on fire. No humiliating or snarky comments. Nothing. Well, except that I had the overwhelming urge to grovel. Maybe suck one of those gorgeous, golden-brown toes while down there.

Gasp! I want to please him? Make him happy? Yes. I longed for lazy-lover weekends of braiding each other's hair and slow roasting tiny, succulent creatures over an open fire while reciting poetry about figs and jam. Okay. Who the hell was I kidding? I wanted to hump like eager bunnies until the wee hours of the morning. In fact, I'd do just about anything for it!

Double gasp!

No one controls Cimil! No one! I have to get the hell out of here! I darted for the door, slammed right into an invisible wall, and fell flat on my back.

Multicolored lights blocked my vision. "What the fuck?" I rubbed my temples.

The man stood over me—yes, yes. Still naked. Gloriously naked. And frowning. "I do not know this word *fuck* you use," he said, "but I assume you are referring to the doorway." He smiled wickedly.

Yes and no. I sat up, feeling the room spin, and in that instant, the man placed a cool, hard object, a collar of sorts, around my neck. It clicked as he clasped it.

Okay. Not the time for gifting, a-hole. "You're delusional if you think a crappy piece of…" I looked down and saw the edge of the thick collar. It was made from several pieces of polished black stone. "A crappy piece of rock is going to appease me." I hopped up and faced off with the large mortal. "And what the hell did you do to the exit?" For the record, there was nothing but open air in that doorway, yet when I'd tried to pass, it had felt like I'd hit a steel wall.

He grinned with deep satisfaction. "I do not answer to you. But know this, you are not leaving this chamber until you submit and vow your loyalty."

What the...? Okay. Now I'm pissed. "Look, you snotty piece of mortal bull crap, I answer to no one. I grovel to no one. And I am not going to braid your hair. Even if you managed to get me a pet sea turtle. Which I would love. But still...it's *not* happening." I poked him in the chest, which was conveniently located at eye level since I was only about five feet tall. "I am the Goddess Cimil. Ruler of the Underworld. I have powers you've never dreamed of. So open that door, or I will suck the soul from that gorgeous bag of bones you call a body and personally deliver it to the fires of hell, where you will burn for eternity."

Okay. For the record, I was pretty sure he didn't know the word *hell*, but I'm sure he got the point. And there really was no official underworld, so to speak; once the dead crossed over from this world, they hung out in this other dimension until ready for their lights to be recycled back into the cosmos.

Some hung out for a really long time—awesome game of poker going down around the clock—others jumped right back into the cosmic soup for another spin in a people suit. I knew one guy who'd done five hundred laps as a goat herder, each time falling off a cliff while taking a nap. Talk about destined to repeat your mistakes! Somebody get that guy a rope!

The king's chest rumbled with a deep chuckle. "You think I do not know who you are, woman? I summoned you. I prayed to the Goddess Bastet to deliver you, a minor goddess, to my bed. You are mine now, and you shall be my queen, the mother to my children."

"Minor!" I burst out laughing and slapped my knee. "Clearly you've been sold a peck of pickled peppers, Peter. First, there's no such Goddess Bastet. She's some made-up deity, loosely modeled after my sister Camaxtli. And if you had any clue about me"—I held my finger up to his nose (gorgeous, strong, straight nose)—"you'd know that I am the most powerful deity in existence. You'd also know that mortals and gods don't mix. We are physically incompatible. Although I'd sure like it if we were, 'cause you look like you'd be some fun. After I spank you and put you in your place, of course. But I digress…" It was time to give him a little taste of my power.

This is gonna hurt! I placed my hand on his chest and willed my gift of pain to channel into his body.

The sensation, for a mortal, was akin to being poked with a hot iron.

He looked down at me with his fierce eyes as I stood there…*Waiting? What the hell?*

I removed my palm, looked at it, and placed it back on his chest. "What did you do, Peter?"

He glanced at the collar around my neck and lifted his chin. "Narmer. My name is Narmer."

"Narmer, Peter, Chucky, Rrrrroberto…who gives a crap?" I roared. "What did you do?"

"Not so powerful after all, are you, Cimil? I own you now. Best accept the idea because you are not leaving this room until you vow eternal fealty to me."

"What? Are you insane! You give me back my powers, you oversized monkey nut!" I tugged at the collar, but it wouldn't come off.

Gasp!

"You can't keep me here!" I screamed.

Minky! Where's Minky? Whatever crap he was pulling, whatever magic he'd used, surely it had been intended for me and not for my trusty unicorn.

I scrambled toward the terrace, immediately sensing yet another barrier separating me from my freedom. *Camel poop!*

I hissed and turned to glare at him.

Okay. Fine. Once Minky got there, I'd make contact and be cloaked by her magic. All right, it's not truly magic per se. Unicorns are simply another highly evolved species, made mostly of energy, similar to us deities when not in our corporal states. The unicorn's current simply flows through anything it touches, making the object or person's particles vibrate so quickly they appear to be invisible to the naked eye. See. Unicorn mystery revealed! Boom.

"Your magical beast is not coming for you," Narmer said from across the room. And once again, that deliciously wicked smile of his made an appearance across those full, sensual lips.

"What?" I asked.

"Your beast is my guest. And you will not see it again until my demands are met."

Jumpin' Mexican beans! Minky! Nooo!

I stomped my foot. "But how…?"

I glared at the man like I've never glared at anyone in my entire existence. How had he known about Minky? Or that I was coming? Who was this guy? How the hell had he trumped me?

I marched over to the bed, sat down with my back to him, and began humming.

"What are you doing?" he asked.

"Outliving you." He could lock me in this room, take away my powers and my precious Minky, but eventually, he would get old and die. He was what? Thirtyish? Humans lived to about forty or fifty in this day and age. I could hang out in his bedroom for a decade or two. No problem. I'd once spent an entire century in a bubble bath. With

Minky, of course. (She makes the best bubbles. Rainbow colored.)

Narmer cleared his throat. "The collar you wear will not come off until I remove it. If you wish to wear it for eternity, then so be it."

He left the room as easy breezy as I'd entered it.

"Son of a bitch!" I'd been one-upped by a mortal.

Where had he obtained such powerful magic? This situation reeked of fishy fish. Yet I was distinctly turned on. *Finally! A male that is my match!*

Chapter Three

Narmer paced across his temporary chamber, cursing the gods. Was this some sort of perverse joke? Seven excruciating days had passed, and that stubborn goddess remained seated on the edge of his bed in the other room, staring outside. She did not move, blink, or speak. Yet he knew she felt acutely aware of his presence; the air was filled with odd vibrations and heat, making the hairs on his arms stand up each time he neared her.

How much longer would she hold out? Surely this was not part of the bargain, the wish of the Goddess Bastet.

Time to ask for help.

"You called, my king?" said the holy man, fat with food and drink, a young woman on each arm.

How any female, even commanded by him, the king, could stomach touching the vile, reptilian man, he did not know. Personally, he'd rather remove his own skin than allow it to come into contact.

Narmer cleared his throat. "Mitnal, I require your assistance. Immediately." He knew asking for this powerful priest's help to again make contact with the gods would come with a steep price. Everything with him did. It was the reason Narmer hoped Mitnal would soon go back to the jungles from where he came.

Twenty moons ago, a mysterious band of no-mads—short in stature, straight black hair the texture of linen threads, high cheekbones, and fat cheeks—passed through Egypt, telling tales of being from the future. They spoke of a magical tablet made of a material called black jade and called themselves the Mayans. They claimed to have built great stone structures that reached high into the sky, allowing them to speak to their gods.

Narmer had not met these travelers personally, but venomous rumors of their greatness spread like wildfire. The Egyptian people began to doubt Narmer's power, doubt that his kingdom was the most favorite of the gods. They began to believe their place in the afterlife was at stake.

Narmer immediately sent two hundred men to bring these Mayans to him, but not a trace was found, only fueling his subjects' speculation of their great abilities. Of course, Narmer did not believe the Mayans were from the future and sent his men back out, commanding them to find these travelers and these lands filled with lush greenery and odd-shaped structures that touched the clouds, which they had spoken of.

Twelve moons later, only one of his soldiers re-turned. According to this man, he'd begun his journey on a small sailing vessel with six others. They'd traveled north, where they encountered a group of golden-haired barbarians who knew of the Mayans. "Across the ocean, where the air is hot and wet, you will find them," they'd said after being coaxed with a bit of gold.

Narmer's men traded for supplies and set out across the ocean, but eventually, their small vessel sank, the other six men lost at sea. It seemed, however, that the gods had been watching out for the one who survived. When he awoke on the sandy white shores of the strange new land, it was a Mayan woman who found him. He went to their village and discovered they were not great at all, but humble farmers and fishermen.

"As I thought!" Narmer had said to his man.

"But my king, I found something else. When I told the Mayans of the band of travelers I sought, they did not know who they were, but they knew of the black jade. One holy man demanded I tell him everything I knew—how the travelers had used the tablet and gotten it to work, from how far in the future they'd come. When I told him I knew nothing, he conjured a great black cloud and wrapped it around my body. I felt fire charring my flesh, and he made me swear to the gods I had told him everything. Then the cloud disappeared."

"Most interesting," said Narmer.

"I've never seen anything like it, my king. Which is why I taught them to make our tools and how to build a small ship with a sail. I have brought the holy man here."

"Here?" Narmer asked.

"Yes, my king. He asks only that we allow him to hear more about his people from the future, what they said, what they wore. Anything. He wants to learn about the magic that brought them here."

"They were not from the future. The holy man is mad," Narmer had said. And he was right. When he met the priest, Mitnal, as he called himself, he looked like a creature from the netherworld. He did not bathe or clean his teeth. He covered himself in the blood of animals and humans. He wore fingers on a string around his neck and smoked strange herbs with a hollow wooden stick. The black cloud his soldier had claimed to have seen must have been the stench. Narmer hoped that showing the madman to the masses—who had been calling for Narmer's dethronement—would dispel all rumors of Narmer not being the favorite son of the gods.

Narmer was about to have the man put on display and then publicly executed when he revealed his magic, producing a bit of rain.

"Where did you learn such powers?" Narmer had asked, but the man simply claimed that his people were born with such gifts, that they were favored by the gods, who often came to visit through their portals.

Naturally, Narmer wondered, *What more can this priest request of the gods?*

Narmer bartered with Mitnal for weeks, granting him anything he wished—small boats, gold, women—in exchange for two things: to publicly declare that the Mayans were but simple people with large imaginations and to deliver Narmer a queen, a divine queen—irrefutable evidence of the gods' favor toward him.

The first request was easy, but the second was not. Mitnal spent night after night burning strange herbs and talking to the souls of the netherworld. "The souls of the dead," he'd said, "can tell us the future." After nearly two moons, Mitnal declared that Narmer's wish would be granted. A goddess would arrive within days, and Mitnal would provide the powerful magic to capture both her body and her heart.

Obviously, that particular piece of the plan had not worked out. And now Narmer would make sure the bargain was fulfilled.

Mitnal dipped his head and flashed a nearly toothless smile. "What assistance do you require, my king? Is all not well with your goddess?"

"The gods granted my wish, just as you predicted. But this…Cimil, she will not submit to me, and she speaks in odd riddles. I think she might be insane." He rubbed his chin. *Hooker? Bigfoot? What strange words the gods speak.* Perhaps these were sacred words, words of power he should inscribe on his tomb. Yes, he would commission a shrine immediately. "In any case, my patience wears thin."

Mitnal shrugged. "She is a goddess. Patience will be required to tame her and make her yours."

Narmer slammed his fist against the cold stone wall. "She is *my* goddess now, and she will receive no more patience from me. Can you assist me or not?"

"I can. But what will you give me in exchange?" Mitnal asked.

More? He wants more! "What do you desire? More gold? Animals?"

Mitnal shook his head. "I have more than I can possibly manage to take back to my lands. I desire something else."

Narmer felt an odd sensation in his gut, as if giant beetles crawled inside him.

"I will tell you how to make the goddess submit," Mitnal said, "but when you have made peace with her and gained her trust, you will tell her about me. You will tell her to trust me."

That sounded simple enough. And truth be told, the goddess did not seem like the sort to trust anyone. He could tell her to trust this smarmy holy man, but she would not.

"Very well. It is a bargain, then. Now tell me how to capture her heart."

Mitnal displayed a venomous grin. "Yes. Capture her heart, we shall."

Chapter Four

Thinking leads to bad places. Why can't I shut it off? I sat on the edge of the bed where I had a clear view of the outside world a few feet away. I don't know how long I stayed there, but not once in all my years had I taken a breath to truly reflect upon my sixty thousand years of existence and what it all meant.

I had worked and worked and worked, hopping from one task to the next, making sure that the souls of the dead didn't hang around too long in the human realm, cluttering up the place and creating a bad vibe. I distracted myself by listening to the dead's stories, to their regrets, to their triumphs and sadness for the people they left behind.

Anyhoo, after ushering tens of millions of souls, the years seemed to blend together into one never-ending story like that thing they call a romance series in the future. But I realized that focusing on my work allowed me to neglect my own woes.

Now I'd taken this forced pause and discovered my life sucked camel balls. I was beyond lonely. I was truly and utterly desolate. I was filled with a gnawing ache deep inside my bones that radiated through every inch of my threadbare soul. If I were to die, there would be no one weeping for the loss. My brethren didn't weep. They didn't laugh, either. Come to think of it, they were just as numb to their misery as I was. Which brought me to my second thought: that vision I saw in Narmer's eyes wasn't a mere vision; it was a sign from the Universe herself. A message.

Why had she chosen him to deliver it? Who the hell knows?

What did it mean? Something bad was coming. No. I didn't mean a remake of *Gigli* or the return of the mullet.

The evil I witnessed in his eyes wasn't the humans tearing apart their planet in a bloody, all-out war or blowing up the world with one of those bomb thingys that I'd heard the dead from ahead speak of. The destruction I saw was us. Us! Yes, as in the deities. The very gods who were created to protect this world end up destroying it, driven mad.

Why?

That was the question. If only I knew. But the Universe had shown me a glimpse of our future, and it was a lonely one.

"Still sitting there, I see?" A deep, masculine voice rumbled against my dark thoughts.

Narmer.

He wore a royal-blue sarong, nothing else, and his hair was tied back with a small golden thong. No. I don't mean underwear. That would be just weird. He'd also shaved off his pharaoh-tee. I normally appreciated men with a little beardage, but he looked clean and fresh and masculine yummy.

Wait! I know! I hopped up from the bed. "Come here!"

His broad shoulders and powerful chest seemed to take up the entire chamber. It was unusual to see such a large human, such a tall human, but they did exist. Clearly. And this one was quite possibly the most divine male specimen I'd ever beheld. He was perfect. Right down to his toasty-brown nipples, rippling stomach, and powerful legs.

I waved him over, but he gave me a look of suspicion.

"Oh, would you stop that?" I said. "I don't bite. Much."

He walked around the bed and stood in front of me. *Well, hello there!* I mentally saluted his milk-chocolaty nipples and then looked up at his face. "Bend down and look into my eyes."

He frowned instead.

Ugh! "Bend, big boy." *Let's see what else the Universe has to say. I'm sure she left me another clue inside that thick skull of yours.*

I saw the anger simmering in his eyes, but he obeyed and slowly lowered his gorgeous face, placing us nose to nose.

I stared deeply into his pupils but only saw what I normally see inside humans: their light and…

Uh-oh. I pulled away.

"What?" he asked.

I stepped back and put on my game face. His light was dull, meaning his end was near. Very, very near. The soul senses such things, and it begins to detach, preparing for the journey ahead.

"What are you doing?" he asked.

Camel crap. I couldn't tell him he was going to die. Besides, there was nothing I could do. It was dangerous to tinker with the natural course of the Universe.

"I know! Let's change subjects!" Better yet, maybe I should try to figure out what the Universe was trying to tell me.

Narmer crossed his beefy arms over his chest. "I grow weary of your riddles. And why are you no longer angry with me?"

"I found something more important to do: I am trying to have an epiphany. A big, big aha moment."

"I do not know these words," he said.

"No. Of course you don't. Because you're not a goddess with mysterious, all-knowing powers, like me." And if those failed, there was always disco dancing to help me relax so the "all-knowing" might come. *Gods, I can't wait for the seventies! Looks like so much fun!* In these times, the humans' idea of a celebration consisted of killing something large, roasting it on a fire, and getting hammered on fermented fruit juice. Lame. I wanted disco balls; really, really big shoes; and wah-wah-wah music.

"Stop!" Narmer barked. "I command you!"

I froze in midlighting finger and turned. "You're ruining my concentration."

He closed the gap between us and grabbed me by the shoulders. I was about to release a surge of light into his hands simply for the sheer joy of watching him shoot across the room and slam into the wall, but then I remembered the stupid collar. I was dead in the water.

"I came to tell you something," he said.

"You may speak."

I could have sworn I saw actual sparks shoot from his eyes. Probably no one had ever told him anything other than "Yes, my king" or "No, my king" and "Your wish is my command, my king." Well, soon he'd be just another soul wondering why he had wasted his life on silly things like wealth and power.

And why the hell he'd messed with me!

He closed his eyes and took a breath, clamping down whatever bull crap he had the urge to say. When his dark eyes opened again, he tilted his head and placed his hand on my cheek. There was flicker of something almost…endearing within them.

"I came to tell you that I am sorry." His jaw muscles ticked as he ground his teeth. "I am sorry for treating you so rudely."

Wow. Looks like that hurt! "Are you okay? Should I make you a pot of soothing chamomile tea or call for a healer?"

His eyes shifted a bit. "I am very well. Why do

you ask?"

Because you look like you just dropped an egg and have the worst PMS ever. "I'm guessing that apologizing, especially to a lowly female, bruised that giant ego of yours. But I'm glad to see you survived. Good stuff. Now, let me go. I have a planet to rescue."

His face turned bright red. "I will not release you until you take the vow."

I rolled my eyes. "Back to square one, are we?"

He didn't respond.

Ugh! "A square is one of those shapes that has four—"

"I know what a square is," he interrupted. "But I do not understand your expression."

"Square one is the place where you started—oh! Never mind, Chucky," I said. "What I meant was that you are infuriating! You thought you could come in here, make an apology—wow! Such a huge sacrifice—and win me over with that? Really, big boy? You've taken me prisoner. You put this collar around my neck like I'm some sort of pet, and you've neutralized my powers. Do you really think an apology is going to—"

He bent his head and kissed me hard.

My entire body lit up like a bonfire, and the heat from his bare chest enveloped me in a steamy wave of lust. My knees buckled, and he immediately wrapped me in his large arms, pulling me close to prevent me from sliding down to the floor, where I conjectured I might end up a squishy little puddle of fluttering nerves and unflattering spasms of joy.

And for a moment, I swore our bodies melted together. I'd never felt anything so potent. That dark, empty space inside my chest began to glow like a warm ember, and the only thing I could think of was stripping away my tiny little top and skirt. I wanted to feel his heavy body slip and slide over mine as his hands and mouth roamed every inch of my—

I pushed away and slapped him. Hard.

Rage flickered in his eyes. "What in the gods' name was that?"

In my name? In my name? I huffed and then poked him. "No! You tell *me* what that was!"

"That was called a kiss."

"Well—well, I know that! But where do you get off kissing me like that? All wet and…" *Dammit, that was a hot kiss. Is this what I've been missing out on?*

The pharaoh quirked a brow. "And what?"

I crossed my arms and looked away. *Yummy. It was yummy.* "Horrible. Worst kiss I've ever had. Were you taught by a camel?"

"A *camel?*" he roared. "I will show you a camel."

The pharaoh reached for me, but I hopped away. "Oh no, you don't! I don't want any of those sloppy humpbacked desert mammal kisses. And you smell like one, too!" He actually smelled delicious, like exotic oils and spices, but the insult felt like a winner, so I went with it.

He chased me around the room. I leaped onto the bed and almost made it to the other side, but his hand snagged my ankle and jerked me back. I lost my footing and fell, flopping onto the bed facedown. He immediately jumped onto my back, pinning my hands above my head, straddling me.

"Let go of me!" I squirmed, but he was much, much larger, and I, powerless without my…um…powers.

"No. Not until you submit."

"Never!" I screamed.

"Then I shall never let you go," he growled.

Stubborn man! I growled back.

He growled again.

I meowed.

He…

…burst out laughing.

Infectious. I'd never heard such a beautifully deep, masculine laugh. Its uninhibited joy sank into my bones and hummed inside my head. It inspired visions of unicorns and rainbows—the natural kind. Not the ones Minky made, which were colorful but not without a strange odor. Anyway, his laugh was pure…*loveliness.*

He rolled off me onto his back, laughing with such ferocity that he could barely breathe. I sat up and watched him, unable to help myself from smiling. He went on and on, like a man who'd not laughed in decades and the dam had finally burst.

"If I'd known the secret to removing that stick from your ass was meowing, I would have started a week ago," I said. "Pinned a tail to my skirt, too."

Tiny tears trickled from the corners of his dark eyes. Thank goodness he didn't wear his ceremonial manliner; otherwise, he'd be a complete mess.

He whisked the tears away, sat up, and looked at me. Not just looked, but beamed. "You are a most peculiar goddess."

"You are one bat-shit crazy pharaoh. And while we're on the subject, exactly why were you laughing?"

He scratched his clean-shaven chin. "I suppose it's the absurdity of the situation. I have spent my entire life on the throne, ruling the people, trusting that the divine blood in my veins would guide me."

Should I tell him he doesn't have any divine blood? Many cultures believed their rulers were descendants of the gods and therefore had the right to rule, but the truth was that they were just normal humans who'd been born at the right time to the right family. *Nahh…let him live his dream.*

"However," he continued, "nothing could have prepared me for this—for you." He reached out and ran his finger along my jaw. "Such a wild creature."

I couldn't stop it from happening. I couldn't. Like he'd been deprived of laughter, I'd been deprived of affection. I'd do just about anything to feel that sensation again, the sensation of being whole. When he'd kissed me, that dark, hollow pit deep inside my chest had filled with something wonderful, something joyous. He was the light inside that dark, damp, wet, and dreary cave I called my heart. I wanted more.

"Kiss me again," I commanded.

His smile melted away and was replaced by a look of raw, carnal hunger. He stared into my eyes as he leaned over and lightly pressed his lips to mine. He slipped his tongue inside and stroked me gently. The warmth of his mouth flooded my face, neck, and chest, eventually making its way deep down inside. For the first time ever, the gears in the old girlie factory started to turn and my female bits ignited.

I jumped on top and straddled his body, kissing him with shameless neediness. I ran my hands over his chest, indulging my urge to worship his masculine form—hard and soft, all in one package.

Speaking of package…

His large shaft lengthened and hardened against my now tingly womanly parts. I moaned. The heat of him felt so sinfully delicious.

He ran his large hands over my breasts. I knew their size and shape would please him; mortal males could never resist gazing at them. Normally, I thought that was silly, but now, knowing my human form excited him, it pleased me.

His hands made their way down to my bare midriff, where he gripped firmly and began rocking me in time to the rhythm of his own hips.

Oh my gods. I think he's starting a fire down there! The delicious friction was more than I could stand. I pulled away from his lips, wanting to see his exquisitely masculine face.

Lids heavy, he looked into my eyes, and…screamed at the top of his lungs!

He threw me, and I tumbled off the bed onto the cold stone floor. "What the hell?"

I peeked over the edge of the bed to see him writhing in pain, cupping the fabric over his penis.

Oops. I forgot to tell him about that. "Um…Narmer." I reached his shoulder and tapped, but he simply rolled back and forth, agonizing.

"Narmer?"

"Aaaah. What?" he groaned.

"About that little raging fire on your totem pole. I, uh—"

"You will pay for this, goddess." He sat up, putting his back to me.

"What?"

His face, beet red, turned toward me. "You think you can make a fool of me, don't you?"

Why…of course I did, but I thought that of everyone! Nuff said. But why had he thought I'd done that on purpose? Had he forgotten he'd put that stupid collar on me? I had no powers. But that didn't mean I could help what I was. My body still radiated concentrated energy. I was a goddess, after all, made of pure light. The form he saw with his eyes was merely a shell that allowed me to enter the physical realm, the realm of humans. But I wasn't human, and he wasn't a deity. We weren't compatible. In fact, prolonged exposure would kill him. Fry him right up like a side of bacon. Crispy king.

There was no getting around it; I was destined to be alone forever.

Still on the floor, I turned away and pulled my knees into my chest, my now empty, dark, heavy chest, and began to cry.

Yes. I know. Deities don't cry. But they do when they realize there is no hope for them.

"More of your trickery, I see," he bellowed. "But your lies and womanly deceits will not work on me."

"Just go! Leave!" I screamed. It was bad enough I was crying. Me, the Goddess of the Underworld!

I heard the shuffle of his feet across the floor as he circled the bed and made his way over. "I command you to stop crying!"

"No!"

He grabbed my arm and pulled me from the floor, gripping me by the shoulders. "Yes. You will. You will cease this attempt to manipulate me and make your vow to me. You will desist this attempt to make a fool of me!"

"You really don't get it, do you?" I barked, trying to wiggle from his grasp. "You've already been made a fool of! I can't be your queen. I can't be anyone's queen. Deities and humans are not compatible. That little 'trick,' as you called it, was just the chemistry of our bodies reacting."

"What is this thing you call 'chemistry'?" he asked.

Ugh. It was a futurist term. "It means that your body is like wood and mine is like lightning. Put us together and they create fire."

He loosened his grip. "You are telling the truth?"

I nodded.

He rubbed his forehead and then turned to leave.

"Wait. Where are you going?" I asked.

"To find magic to fix this." He disappeared through the doorway.

I dropped my head and made tiny circles with my fingertips over my temples. "What are you doing, Cimil? He's going to die soon, and you're playing fantasy hookup! With a mortal." I sighed loudly. Not because I was disappointed at myself, but because there was no magic to fix this, and for the first time ever, I really wanted something I couldn't have: a human. A human who was about to expire and would likely end up being one of those stubborn-ass souls I had to drag to the other side by the earlobes, kicking and howling the entire way.

This situation screamed tragedy.

"I must be crazy, bat-shit crazy."

Chapter Five

Carrying his favorite knife, Narmer burst into the priest's bedchamber, startling the old man and the three women who were nude and apparently giving him a full-body massage before bedtime.

Disgusting. How can they bear to touch him? Narmer resisted retching.

"Out! All of you!" Narmer roared at the women, who grabbed their dresses and fled.

The priest scrambled from his bed and placed his back against the wall. "Now, calm down, my king. I'm sure this is simply some misunderstanding."

"You tricked me! And I am not your king! You are not worthy of being even my lowliest subject. I am your executioner!" Narmer pushed the long knife to the man's neck.

The priest clawed at Narmer's hand. "You are upset, I see," the priest croaked.

"The goddess is unable to lie with me. She says we are not physically compatible—fire and wood." Narmer bounced the man's back against the wall. "I swear by the gods, you will fix this!"

"I cannot."

"Cannot or will not?"

"Cannot," Mitnal said. "You may kill me, but what you ask is something I do not have the power to give. My magic is not strong enough."

Narmer released the man and ran his hand over his hair. He needed a divine queen. He needed to have heirs. He wanted Cimil. Her sharp tongue and obstinate ways made her more alluring than any female he'd ever met, and there had been many. In his earlier years, he would bed two or three women each night. They lined up outside his door, hoping to be the one to permanently catch his eye or mother his child. But the gods had not willed it, and he saw nothing in these women except greed for his wealth and power. They left him feeling hollow, unsated, and more frustrated than when he started. That was why he eventually came to the conclusion that only a female his equal, a truly unique and powerful female, would suit him. Of course, being who he was, the ruler of the most glorious and advanced civilization known to all, meant that no one equaled him. He had the blood of the gods running in his veins. Yes, only a full-blooded goddess would do.

"If what I ask is beyond your powers," Narmer said, "does this mean you know of another way?"

The evil man smiled an evil grin.

"Name your price," Narmer commanded.

The priest laughed nervously. "The price is far too high."

"I will kill you right here and now if you do not tell me."

"Very well," Mitnal said, "the price is your life."

He was mad. "I am fairly certain that my death would not solve the issue."

"You will not truly die, but be born again into another form, one that can withstand the touch of a deity. You will be strong and immortal, almost as resilient as a true god."

"How do you know this?" Narmer asked.

"My people have long pursued immortality."

This sounded dangerous. If the gods wished humans to live forever, then they would have created them in such a way. "This is impossible."

Mitnal held up his hands and wiggled his filthy fingers. "No. Not impossible. I have already succeeded with small creatures. We merely lack the power to make a human immortal." His eyes widened into horrifying orbs of black and red. "You can change that."

Narmer stepped back. *The man is a vile, deceitful creature.* He did not trust this Mitnal. There was some ulterior motive lurking inside the man's head. But what? Did he want the throne? Narmer's gold? Perhaps he could persuade the crazy man to disclose his true plans.

"What must I do?" Narmer asked.

"You must gain her trust and then convince her to come see me, to trust me."

Again with this request? Mitnal had this

planned all along. He was after stronger magic. Deity magic.

"And what assurances do I have," Narmer asked, "that you will not use her in some way to make yourself more powerful and then refuse to assist me?"

The priest rubbed his greasy palms together. "You have my good word, my king."

Disgusting, filthy pile of rotting monkey meat. Whatever plan the priest had, helping Narmer was only a means to an end.

"She will not trust you," he said. "She trusts no one. Find another way for me to bed her. I give you eight days."

The next week was unlike anything I'd ever experienced in my sixty-five thousand years. The pharaoh would come each evening after his bath, face meticulously shaved—an Egyptian obsession— his tanned skin and perfectly chiseled muscles gleaming with fragrant oils, his long black hair washed and braided. I began to wonder about the females who attended him. Were they young and beautiful? Did they offer up their nubile bodies and provide him the pleasures of the flesh I could not? (Nipple tweaking, back waxing, deep pore cleansing.) My fists curled each time I visualized those little Tut-sluts massaging his enormous sarcophagus or playing with his treasure chest. My only consolation was that they were not getting what I had, his adoration.

We spent each night discussing the confines of our lives, the boundaries and expectations that created an invisible prison we could not escape. He would lie next to me and tell stories of his deceased mother and father, of his twenty-five siblings (all but five of them half-siblings) and how their one mission in life, when growing up, was to escape the watchful eye of their guards for a few precious moments of mischief and recreation. He spoke of how empty his life became the moment he realized his brothers and sisters would turn on him if given the chance to rule in his place.

I talked about my world, the souls I escorted, and of my brethren. I recounted my first memories of consciousness, vaguely realizing what I was, but not understanding the full weight of the eternal shackles binding me to the Universe.

We kissed and touched many times each night, only stopping when my energy became too intense for him or when I felt the need to recite a haiku. About a sea turtle. (Don't ask.)

Each time he broke free, I saw the torment in his eyes. Not only was he denied his pleasure, but also his male ego did not enjoy leaving me wanting—it reminded me of the Home Shopping Network. Then he would fall asleep next to me, and I would drift off to the netherworld, hearing the voices of the dead laughing and howling as they played poker. I'd never felt closer or such an intimate connection with anyone in my entire life.

Heaven. He was my little slice of man-succulent heaven.

When Narmer entered on the seventh night, however, I knew something was wrong. He hadn't had his usual bath, and his skin was covered with desert dirt and sweat. He paced across the room at the foot of the bed.

"What?" I asked.

"I cannot bear this any longer," he growled.

"Bear what?"

His head snapped in my direction. "This!"

I rolled to my side and propped my head up on my arm. "Care to elaborate? Because if you're tired of being in this room, then all you need to do is lift the spell. While you're at it, you can remove my collar, too." I shrugged. "Who knows, maybe I'll find a way to show my gratitude." I popped my index finger in my mouth and sucked in a suggestive manner.

Okay, so I couldn't do that without setting the royal totem pole on fire, but the thought alone made me start to sweat. I wanted this man. I wanted him so badly that my toenails throbbed. But more importantly, I wanted to enjoy him every second I could get. He would die soon.

Don't get me wrong, I'd thought about ways to help him, but the only means of saving a mortal was to take them to my world and saturate them with the light of the gods. I'd have to convince my brethren to allow this, and they hadn't granted this gift in twenty thousand years. They were like stubborn children who didn't want to share their candy. If I went against them, they would banish me forever. Or, at the very least, for a really, really, really, really, reeeeally long time. That said, I was almost ready to roll the dice and do it anyway. I simply wanted a sign. A teeny tiny sign that this was what I was supposed to do.

Narmer's body visibly pulsed with tension. "I want you, Cimil. I want you very much. When I asked the gods for a queen, a true goddess, I hoped for a female I could respect. One who might be intelligent and powerful to help me rule, but you..." He marched over to the bed, his eyes sweeping over my stretched-out body. "You are all that and more. I would give anything to lie with you as a man lies with a woman."

"Ah, sexual frustration. My constant companion." I nodded my head, knowing exactly how he felt. "But didn't you say you had your secret friend working on a solution? By the way, you never told me his name, but I'd like to meet him; he's got some pretty rockin' juju. However, he is in need of a very long spanking for assisting you in your plot to capture me."

I looked up at Narmer's body. Every muscle quaked and trembled with agitation.

"Oh, my little love turnip is upset. Shall I meow for you?" I clawed the air.

"This is no joke, Cimil. I lost my temper today

with one of my brothers. He and his followers have been positioning themselves for years, trying to raise an army to overthrow me. They say my dream of unifying our people is impossible, that I am mad!"

I shrugged. "Tell them to pound sand. There's plenty of that around here—should keep 'em busy for a while."

"I do not know this expression, but I assume you mean I should send them elsewhere." Narmer dropped his head. "I should have done that, but I did not."

Uh-oh. "What did you do?"

"I beat my brother in front of my entire council."

That was when I noticed his bloody knuckles. *Ouch.* "Is he alive?" 'Cause Narmer was huge. I mean huuuuuge. I couldn't imagine that many would survive a thumping from the king himself.

"Yes. But he has sworn his revenge. This is exactly the spark they hoped for. War is imminent."

I felt the internal conflict bubbling in my chest. I wanted to tell Narmer to let his brother have the kingdom, to run away with me and enjoy what little time he had left. But I knew in my heart that my telling him the truth would create the opposite effect. Humans tended to spiral into a state of depression when they knew death neared. Narmer would spend his final days feeling defeated and miserable.

The only option was to kidnap him and petition

the gods to make him immortal. "I will help you, Narmer, but you must free me," I said.

He stared at me. "You will make the vow?"

What the hell? "We're back to this again? Seriously, Narmer?" I popped up from the bed and got in his face—errr, well—chin. I got in his chin. He was really tall. "You stupid, arrogant, insane—"

He reached down and cupped the back of my head and pulled me into him for a deep, needy kiss. My body melted against his delicious male heat.

He slowly pulled away and gazed into my eyes. "I am unable to remove the barrier or the collar, even if I so desired, my love. You are the only one who holds the key to breaking the spell."

So the little devil had lied to me. He could not remove it. Sneaky, little pharaoh. *Gods, I think I love this man.*

"However," he added, "if it will make you feel more comfortable, I will first make my vow to you." Once again he kissed me deeply, passionately. My mind swirled with new emotions and with a fire I'd quickly and irrationally become addicted to. I'm pretty damned sure his lips were feeling the fire, too. Touching me for any length of time was no fun.

He kneeled and stared up with his dark eyes.

"What are you doing?" I asked.

"I, Narmer, son of Ka and king of Egypt, vow to you, Cimil, Goddess of the Underworld, my eternal soul, my eternal loyalty, my eternal love—"

I blinked and Narmer was on his side, blood

oozing from his chest, a giant spear sticking from
him.

I pivoted on my heel and saw two men standing
in the doorway, one with his arm cocked, ready to
throw another spear. I reached toward the small
table at the side of the bed, grabbed a vase, and
threw it right at his head. It landed with a loud
crack and the man dropped. The second man
scrambled for the spear and came at me. I ducked
and spun, avoiding the razor-sharp tip of his spear,
and ended up behind him.

*Sorry, buddy, but in my sixty-five thousand years,
one thing I've learned is how to fight.* I grabbed the
man from behind, wishing I could reach inside him
and yank out his fucking soul; however, I still didn't
have my powers. Instead, I settled for hanging on
tight and letting nature take its course. In this case,
that meant allowing my energy to flow into his
body. The man howled and dropped to the floor,
his body smoking. I picked up the spear and ran it
straight through his heart. *Evil bastard.*

I looked over at Narmer, who hacked blood into
crimson puddles.

"No. Oh, gods, no!" That was when I realized
that I wasn't ready to let him go. Not now. Not
ever. I couldn't imagine a future, an eternity
without him by my side. It was like discovering
cheesecake and finding out the only chef in the
world who knew how to make it had jumped off a
cliff. Narmer made life taste so good, and I wanted

more. He understood me. He saw me for who I really was, yet he still loved me, wanted me.

I kneeled next to him. "Don't leave me, you bastard." My mind raced through the solutions but found only one. I would have him free Minky. We'd dart off to my portal, and I would take him back to my world. Damn the gods if they didn't agree with my choice to grant him immortality. What was the point of being a goddess if I couldn't use the tools given to us by the Universe?

"Narmer, honey." I stroked back the dark locks from his face. "Tell me where you put Minky."

Narmer groaned. "Are you going to leave me now that I am dying?"

"No, you silly man, I am going to save you."

"Your creature was taken to the Temple of Bastet."

Camel crap. That was on the other side of the city.

"You might not live that long. Dammit all to hell! There has to be another way."

Something flickered in his eyes. "If you see Mitnal, whatever you do..." Narmer's eyes rolled into his head and he passed out.

Oh my gods. Oh my gods. He only had minutes at best; I had to do something.

"I, Yum Cimil, Goddess of the Underworld, vow eternal loyalty to you, Narmer, pharaoh of Egypt. For as long as I live, my heart and soul belong to you and no other. I love you. I love you.

Please don't die," I cried.

My collar fell to the floor, and my body buzzed with divine energy.

I'm free!

I cracked the spear sticking from his body and pulled it out so I'd be able to carry him over my shoulder. But there was so much blood.

Fuck, fuck, fuck. I pulled strips of fabric from the bedding and tried to plug the hole, but the blood came too fast.

I flung him over my shoulder, grateful for the return of my powers, which included physical strength, and fled the chamber. Dead bodies were strewn about the temple, and it was obvious Narmer's guards had taken down a few of his brother's men before losing the battle to defend their king.

I scampered down the steps of Narmer's private temple, feeling his warm blood trickling down my lower back and legs. Oh, gods, he wasn't going to make it!

I ran straight through the courtyard toward the outer temple that led to the exit, but standing there was a strange, little man. He wore a loincloth and necklace made of human fingers. His hair was pulled into a strange, little ponytail atop his head. He reeked of dark energy, like he'd bathed in evil.

Ugh! It's one of those creepy Mayan priests! I knew this because (a) we bumped into his peeps quite often given our portals were in their barrio and (b) because these tiny bastards had recently decided that ripping out people's hearts was a spiffy way to amp up their powers. Remember that River of Tlaloc I talked about? Well, his people had been drinking the damned water for so long, they'd developed supernatural powers. Mostly harmless ones—seeing the dead, making rain, talking to animals, blah, blah, blah—but they were certainly on our deity radar.

"What the hell are you doing here?" I asked.

He held out his hand to stop me. "He will die, but I can help you save him."

I blinked as my mind tried to sort out the pieces. "Mitnal, I presume."

He smiled and flashed his blackened teeth. "Why, yes, my dear goddess." He bowed. "At your service."

"Good. I need to get across town to the Temple of Bastet. I need to get back to my cenote."

Mitnal slowly shook his head as if he'd achieved some sinister victory. My goddess red flags were flying their colors high in the sky. In fact, if I weren't so busy, I'd snatch the soul right out of him. He was bad news.

"You will never make it in time," he said. "He is turning blue. If I may, my goddess, offer another suggestion. One that is guaranteed to save our dear pharaoh?"

What had Narmer been trying to tell me before he'd passed out? It had sounded like a warning.

Well, I didn't need a warning. Anyone could see this man was up to no good.

"He has stopped breathing," Mitnal pointed out.

I stilled. *Dammit, dammit, dammit.* I slid Narmer down on the ground and started doing that thing called CPR. Humans in the future had developed the technique, and it did save lives on occasion.

"Whatever it is, do it!" I screamed between puffing breaths into Narmer's bloody mouth.

Mitnal sank to his knees. He reached his arms high in the sky and began reciting a prayer to the Universe, a prayer to summon the dark energy. Like a godsdamned evil magnet, evil light collected around him and began to swirl around us, kicking up dust and leaves.

Great, fucking great. The crazy priest is going to save him with evil dirt!

"I call to the gods, to the divine Creator of all life," Mitnal chanted, whipping his arms around, spinning the dark energy into tight circles.

Damn. What is he doing?

Mitnal looked at me. "Rise to your knees, goddess!" he screamed.

I did as he asked, covering my ears. The noise was deafening.

"You have vowed to give your heart to this man, yes?" Mitnal asked.

"Yes! Yes." I had such a bad feeling about this.

"Then in the name of the divine Creator." He reached out with his long, blackened fingernails and plunged his hand into my chest, pulling from it my beating heart. I looked at the human organ, unable to react or speak. Mitnal held the heart in the air, and the dark energy whooshed inside it, disappearing. "With this divine spark of life, the blood of the pharaoh shall live forever."

He plunged my heart into Narmer's chest, and the sky burst with lavender. I felt my light flicker.

I held my hand over the gaping hole in my chest. "What have you done?" I hissed.

Mitnal grinned. "I saved him, just as you asked. With a piece of your light. And soon, my people will have an immortal army with which we will conquer the world. We will be the greatest civilization ever to rule."

A black splotch spread across my line of sight, and then death swallowed me whole.

In a rage, I emerged several days later from the Mexican cenote. That's where deity souls end up when our human bodies are destroyed. From there, we can choose to return to our realm or have the cenote provide us with a new human suit.

In this case, I'd opted for a new body. Not only did I want revenge, but also I needed to know if Narmer was all right. And I wanted answers. Because while my new humanlike body, which included a new heart, felt fine, my light felt slightly weaker.

I immediately set out for the Mayan village just a few hours away by foot. I would find one of Mitnal's cohorts and torture the truth from them. What horrible, dark magic were they using? Why did they believe it would create an immortal army? But when I arrived, the village leader said that the priests had disappeared many moons ago. No one knew where they were. One could only assume somewhere in the jungle, planning world domination. *Idiots.*

As soon as I knew Narmer was all right, I would call a summit and propose the gods take action. The priests would have to be taken out.

Chapter Six

One year later…
(Yep, still somewhere around 3000 BC.)

Clothes tattered, hair matted into giant, platypus-tail-like clumps, skin charred and covered in grime of the most unimaginable sorts, I schlepped my way up the steps of Narmer's temple. My new human-like heart pounded like a war drum inside my chest, mirroring the roar of thunder booming through the air. Rain and lightning showered down on everything around me. I couldn't stop it; my overflowing emotions had to be released somewhere. Gods, what I'd been through this past year. All just to make it back to Egypt. Back to my beloved Narmer. I could only hope he was all right.

I stopped at the entrance of the outer temple and looked around. Where were Lefty and Righty? Granted, they'd likely been killed during the attack on that fateful night one year ago; however, I would have expected the pharaoh to have a new set of hunky-skirts guarding his door. Yet there was no one. In fact—I turned and looked back toward the muddy avenue bathed in the gray light of the fading day—the crowded scene of merchants carrying their goods had been replaced by an utter lack of human life. Where had everyone gone?

Goose bumps erupted on my skin, and the air became electrified with dark energy. *Oh, gods, please let him be all right,* I prayed.

I entered the dank, dark temple and quietly made my way through the maze of chambers that would lead to the inner courtyard. The place was a damned mess. Broken vases, dirt, leaves, and sand covered the once pristine stone floors. Dried-out weeds sprouted alongside wilted potted plants.

What had happened?

"Narmer?" I called out as I reached the foot of his private temple.

No response.

If that godsdamned Mitnal did anything to him, I'd rip out the man's innards with a spork. No, those wouldn't exist for thousands of years until the colonel blessed the planet with a socially acceptable reason to publicly lick one's fingers; however, I'd find some creative way to pass the time until such sporks were available to carry out my revenge. Torture was a good time-passer-byer.

I made my way up the steps, trying to ignore my throbbing, cracked feet and the aches and pains jabbing each muscle of my shivering humanlike body.

Almost to Narmer's private bedchamber, a muted whimper caught my attention.

"Narmer?" I whispered. The coppery scent of fresh blood filled my nostrils. I reached the doorway and looked inside. My heart sank as my eyes registered the scene before me: Narmer. On the bed with three naked women. The body of one dangled off the edge, her eyes vacant with death and a dribble of blood running down the side of her neck onto the floor. The second woman lay with her wrist wedged into Narmer's mouth, and the third— well, the third moaned beneath him as he pumped himself between her thighs.

"What the…?" I gasped.

Narmer's head lifted, and he stared like a wild beast, continuing the rhythm of his hips. "What the fuck do you want?"

My heart cracked in two. "I-I…" I didn't know what to say.

The woman beneath him reached up, grabbed his hair, and yanked his face toward her demanding lips. The other female, the one who was still alive, obviously, grunted like a cavewoman and shoved her wrist between them, back into his mouth. All the while, Narmer continued hammering.

I turned away. I couldn't bear to look. I couldn't bear to let him see me crumble into a million pieces. I didn't know what he'd become, but that was not the man I'd spent the last twelve months fighting to return to. It had taken me six tries, six bodies to cross the ocean. Each time I died, my light returned to the cenote in Mexico. But I hadn't given up. It was the worst, most excruciating year of my existence, not knowing if he was all right. The fear, the sorrow, the panic consumed me to a point that I'd had no choice but to cut myself off from my brethren completely, lest the gods be overcome with my grief.

I stumbled out of Narmer's temple, fisting my hand over the gaping, raw hole in my chest. Yes, my new body had a new heart, but that mad holy man had ripped away part of my soul and given it to Narmer. The ironic part was that these past months, I'd found comfort in the hope that Narmer might feel a connection and know I was making my way to him.

I am such a fool. I'd believed that he truly cared for me. I believed that when he'd taken that vow, it had actually meant something.

But it hadn't. Or if it had, the Narmer who'd cared for me no longer existed. I could not begin to process the overwhelming despair, the anger, the confusion over what I'd seen. It was too much. I had to bury it, lock it up where it couldn't hurt me.

I made my way across the small city to the Temple of Bastet, hoping I'd find Minky. I'd set her free and retreat back to the cenote, back to my world. But what would I tell my brethren?

That I fell in love with a mortal and then allowed some decrepit Mayan priest to turn him into a monster with my light?

I entered the eerily vacant temple and began

searching the chambers. One, two, three empty chambers. "Godsdammit! Minky! Where are you?" I needed to get out of there. I needed to run from the pain.

"You will not find her here." Narmer appeared out of thin air right before my eyes, dressed in a simple piece of cloth wrapped around his waist.

I shrank back. "What *are* you?"

He smiled and wiped away the fresh blood still stuck to his lips. "What are *we*?" he corrected.

"We?"

"Oh yes, there are many of our new species. My five brothers and sisters were affected by Mitner's evil sorcery. I can only assume because we are connected by our blood. Of course, the struggle for power began almost immediately, so each of us has created children. My army grows the fastest because I am the strongest."

"Army?" Great. What had I done? I needed to get the hell home and tell my brethren. I needed to get the hell out of there before I had a breakdown. The man I loved was dead. Dead! Replaced by this cold, power-hungry monster. "My blessings to you and your new scary family. Where's my unicorn?"

Narmer snarled in my face. "Where the fuck were you?"

"Me? Oh, you know. Here. There. I found a couple of hotties down in the Caribbean," I lied. "If the palm tree is a-rocking, don't come a-knockin'. Where. The. Hell. Is. Minky?"

Narmer slammed me against the wall, knocking the breath from my body. "Your beast is dead."

Bastard. "You can't kill a unicorn; they're made of pure light."

"I had Mitnal fix that, right before I sucked the blood from his body. Then I drank your little unicorn, too. She was"—he sucked in a breath—"delicious."

Motherfucker! "That's impossible. You're lying!"

"Impossible? Impossible," he screamed. "Look at me! Look what you have done to me! Nothing is impossible."

"But I…" I didn't know what to say. I wasn't about to admit that I'd loved him and tried to save him. "I think you got what you deserved for fucking with a goddess." *And killing my Minky!*

I turned away. But then another thought hit me. He was evil. I was a goddess. I could undo the wrong and make it all right. This was not the man I'd loved. This was some dark, twisted version of him.

I reached out my hand, calling on my gift of soul claiming, and placed it on his chest. I'd take back what was given to him.

Nothing.

I stared at him. He stared back, apparently pleased with himself.

"Looking for something?" he asked.

"Your soul? It seems to be missing."

"I'm dead! I have no soul for you to claim, goddess. You lose."

Smug jerk! I slapped him across the face. Now, normally that would send a man flying across the room. But not Narmer. His head barely moved. And my hand kind of hurt.

"You cannot injure me," he said. "I am strong. I am immortal. Just like you."

He gripped my shoulders, pulled me into him, and kissed me hard. I squirmed and released a surge of energy to ward him off. It did absolutely nothing.

He broke the kiss and laughed.

"Let me go!" I wailed.

He did and then bowed his head. "As you wish, my goddess."

"This isn't over, and once the other gods learn of you—and they will—you will be exterminated."

His eyes glittered with arrogance. "By now, I am certain they already know. Your brother Kinich happened to make an appearance the day I was transformed. He spent many months with me, studying our new species. He did not seem bothered by us at all. To the contrary, we've become quite the best of friends."

What? Kinich approved of these soul-sucking demons? "I don't believe you. Kinich is kind and sensitive. He'd never—"

"He sees us as proof that change is possible." Narmer casually waved his hand through the air. "He is inspired by our kind. So much so that he's returned to take his rightful place as your leader to bring forth a new era."

"You're lying," I scoffed.

"You do not need to take my word. Ask him."

"Oh, I will! You can bet on it, bub! After I take your head!" I lunged, and he threw me to the floor, pinning me beneath him.

Rage flickered in his eyes. "You are so weak. What did I ever see in you?" he growled.

"You *saw* something you'll never have. You're not good enough for a goddess. You never were. And now, you're nothing but a lowly, bloodsucking insect, no better than a leech or mosquito."

"Can a mosquito do this?" He moved so fast that all I saw was the blur of his hand as I felt my head detaching from my body.

Son of a bitch! The rat bastard actually removed my head. Sure, I'd tried to suck the soul from his body and end him, but that was after I had seen that he'd apparently killed that woman by draining her dry and confessed to murdering Minky.

Revenge. It pounded inside my mind, demanding to see the light of day. Revenge was the reason I'd elected to have the cenote create yet another body and spit me out rather than return me to my realm, where I was certain my brethren wondered what had become of me. Revenge had replaced every ounce of love I held for Narmer.

What had I been thinking to become so absorbed in this man? I had behaved like a love-starved child, jumping at the first person who came along offering affection.

I'd bet my life that he'd put the evil priest up to the entire thing. A trap. Well, I would never fall for that again. Never. And I would have my revenge. That I vowed.

I crawled from the cenote and flopped down onto the moist dirt of the jungle floor. I listened to the sound of my breath, the sound of my heart, the birds chirping noisily above. *I will find a way back, and I will kill him. Yes, this time I will come prepared.*

Crossing that frigging ocean again in a stolen dinghy?

Ugh. I groaned. Why couldn't humans invent faster? I'd happily take the frigging Christopher Columbus *Santa Maria* special! And that ship would be a rat-infested piece of crap once it came along.

I should've gone back to my realm to find out what Kinich really knew.

I rolled over onto my back.

"Hello."

I yelped as my eyes registered...*Me?*

"What the hell?" I scrambled back doing a strange little crab crawl as I looked her over. Her dress was pink, shiny, and clearly from the future.

"Yeah," the Other-me said, with one fist cocked on her hip. "I figured you'd freak out. But let me assure you, it only goes downhill from here."

"What the hell?" Maybe I'd tripped through the cenote one too many times, or there'd been a malfunction. "What the *hell?*"

"I think you said that already, so why don't you shut your piehole so I can explain. Can you do that?"

I nodded slowly.

"Good, because I'm only going to tell you this once. You have fucked up. Big. Time. You stupid, horrible, pathetic goddess." She cackled. "I've always wanted to say that."

This had to be the most twisted thing I'd ever done to myself.

Okay. Time to end this little imaginary chat. I stood up and started to back away.

"Don't make me pull out the big guns, Cimil. 'Cause I will. You know I will," Other-me said.

"I don't have time for this! I've got a bloodsucking pharaoh to kill. I'm going back to the cenote—" I looked at the watery portal, but instead of seeing a greenish pool, I saw bodies. Thousands of them piled high and overflowing.

I gasped and turned, only to see a wall of people staring right through me with extremely unhappy faces. Mixed in these faces were…"Guy? Chaam? Kinich…Ixtab!" What were all thirteen gods doing there?

I waved my hands in front of their faces, but they didn't seem to acknowledge my presence.

"I'm losing my crazy-loca head," I whispered.

"Nope. They can't see you. They're all dead," Other-me said.

"Nope," I argued. "I'm crazy. Do you know how I know that? Because I'm standing here talking to myself!"

Other-me held out her hand and hit me with a powerful surge of numbing light. Every major muscle froze.

Dammit. That's one of my best tricks!

"Cimil, you will listen very carefully. Do you understand? Make like a dashboard hula girl if you do."

"Huh?"

She rolled her eyes. "Nod! Nod if you understand."

I managed to make a little nod.

"Good," she said, "because as you are aware, the souls of the dead reside in a place beyond the confines of time and space."

She released her grip, and I sucked in some air. "Yes. And I am the only one who can open a portal between the worlds…"

The Other-me jumped up and down, clapping. "Ding, ding, ding! You got it! I opened it up so we could have a little chat."

I pointed to her. "Wait. So this isn't a dream?"

"Nope. I'm dead! So is everyone else." She looked at my brethren, whose empty eyes made it easy to see that something horrible had happened to them. "And it was all your fault!" She looked up at the sky and kept on looking.

"Hello?" I snapped my fingers. "Helloooo?"

She didn't respond.

Gods, the future version of me was so annoying. What happened?

"Hey! Wake up!"

She snapped to. "Hi there!" She smiled with wide eyes.

"You were explaining that I did something wrong?" I asked.

"Aha!" She flicked up her index finger. "Therein lies the question." She shook her head and let out a whoosh. "I don't have a clue."

"You don't know?" I asked.

She shook her head. "I know we all went crazy and basically blew up the planet. Oh! And that it's your fault."

Just like the vision I'd seen in Narmer's eyes! Except for the it-being-my-fault part.

"You're trying to tell me," I said, "that I did something wrong, but you don't know what. And that whatever this thing is, I destroyed the planet? So how do you know it was me?"

"I remember dancing around the large hall, singing, 'I won! It's finally over!' Other than that, it's pretty much a blank."

"That's not proof! Come on!"

She stared with a deep frown. "Okay, I do remember one more thing—well, two, really—but one is pretty depressing. Not sure I should go there."

"Please, go there."

"Okay." She clapped excitedly. "I remember sleeping with a lot of strange creatures. What did you call that pharaoh?"

"A bloodsucker."

She touched her nose. "That's it! I remember sleeping with a lot of bloodsuckers. I mean"—she fanned her face—"*a lot*! But something was always missing."

A soul, perhaps? "So this is your big depressing clue?" I asked.

"No. That's the happy memory. Several thousand years from now, you discover that you are actually the bringer of the apocalypse." She sighed. "This is how the Creator designed you."

That couldn't be right. I always protected humanity, safeguarded them from destruction. Except when I felt the need to deliver pain to the stupid, humiliate the weak, destroy all things imperfect— *gasp! That's, like, everyone. Except for me. And Minky, of course.*

I covered my mouth, unable to believe it. "I am the bringer of the apocalypse?" I whispered.

"See. I told you. Completely sucks. I didn't want to go there," said Other-me.

"But why? Why would the Creator want this? Why would he-she make me evil?"

She shrugged. "How the hell am I supposed to know? That's like asking why evil even exists. Or why lions like to chow down on baby gazelles. It's like asking why humans created *Teen Mom* and call it entertaining. Bad, tasteless things are simply a part of the equation. Evil is a necessary ingredient."

I understood that. I did. After all, I was a goddess. There could be no life without death. There could be no joy without first understanding sorrow. No enlightenment without suffering. But I didn't feel evil. I felt good. Okay, good with a really mischievous streak.

"This can't be right." I shook my head.

"Look at the evidence," she said. "Everything you do, even with good intentions, always ends in a mess."

"Noooo," I protested.

She folded her pale arms.

"Oh, really? What about the Festival of Lights?" she asked.

"Okay. But how was I supposed to know that the volcano would erupt and kill all those people?" I squabbled.

"And Atlantis?" she said condescendingly.

"Plato completely exaggerated that story! It was a practical joke! Besides, Máax forgave me for sinking his island."

Other-me stared.

Hell. Maybe she's right. I thought about Narmer and how I'd inadvertently created an evil new species that dined on people.

"Okay. Fine," I admitted. "I seem to have a destructive streak, but what do I do?" I asked. Because despite everything, I didn't want the world to end, and I certainly didn't want to cause the death of my brothers and sisters.

"Be evil," she replied.

"Brilliant plan." I sat in the dirt and covered my face, groaning.

"You do realize you're naked and getting mud in your butt crack, right?"

I growled at Other-me. "Who the hell cares?" We were all going to die anyway. Dirty and clean butt cracks alike.

She plunked down next to me. "I care, and so do you. That's why instead of protecting humanity, you will try to destroy it."

What exactly was Other-me smoking? Unicorn turds? Oh yes, laugh if you like, but no one has ever recovered from such a journey.

"Great plan. Really, I mean it," I said. "But I think I'll go back to my realm and consult with my brethren." I stood up, brushed the dirt from my ass, and started toward the cenote, which was no longer piled with bodies—that little trick had only been a way to get my attention, I assumed.

"No. You mustn't tell them," she protested, stepping in front of me. "They will only think you've gone insane and see you as a threat to humanity. They will lock you away."

"What do you propose I do?" I asked.

"I'm serious. You will fight your instincts to help or do good. Whatever you think is right, you will do the exact opposite. Voilà. No more destruction!"

"You're an idiot."

Other-me gripped my shoulders. "No. You're an idiot! Okay, which makes me an idiot, too. But you have to do this."

I shook my head no. "If I did the opposite of everything I felt was right, men would be deported to the moon. Especially Egyptian men. Named Narmer." *Hey. Not a bad idea!*

Other-me stomped her foot. "Cimil, this isn't a joke."

"Who's joking?"

She gave me the infamous Cimil stare of death. I'd invented it several centuries ago. Glad to know I'd not given it up. It was very scary.

"You're not even sure this will change the future," I grumbled. "Who's not to say that me trying to destroy the world doesn't end with me actually destroying it?"

"You have a point," she said, tapping her finger on the side of her mouth. "If only we had a sign from the Universe."

I cringed.

"Ha! I know that look!" She jumped up and down pointing at me. "You got a sign, didn't you?"

Yes. I'd seen the vision in Narmer's eyes. "I saw a glimpse of the gods going insane and destroying the world." I sighed. "Because they are lonely."

"Ha! I'm right! I knew it." She hugged me. "Cimil, you must find them all soul mates. While doing the opposite of trying to do anything good, of course. In fact, you should start with yourself. Go find your man!" She started doing that little dance from the future called disco, and I resisted the urge to join along. Disco dancing always made me feel better.

"Love is not in the cards for me. Never has been, never will be."

"Sorry, but the Universe has spoken." She went into lightning-finger mode. A timeless disco-move classic.

"The man I thought I loved crushed my heart and ripped off my head. Oh, he's also turned into some dark, scary creature that drinks blood."

The only, and I mean only, thing I wanted to do was get my ass back to Egypt to dish out a little payback.

"You have to make up with him," she said happily.

"Not gonna happen. I hate the man. I will never love again."

"You must learn to forgive," she pushed.

I looked her squarely in the eyes. "He killed Minky."

"Motherfucker! If everyone wasn't dead already, I'd kill the bastard," she replied.

Damned right! And what a damned strange conversation.

"Then you will have to focus on our brethren and get them to fall in love," she said. "While you do the opposite of anything you think is in the best interest of humanity. So you can save us, of course."

I laughed so loud that the leaves from the trees above shook violently. "That's even crazier than asking me to fall in love."

I didn't mean it as an insult, but did she realize who we were talking about? There was my sister Ixtab, Goddess of Suicide. She would scare mortal man right out of his skin. Then there was my brother Votan, the God of Death and War. His ego was so big I often wondered how he managed to squeeze it into a mortal form. Then there was Kinich, God of the Sun and our leader. He was so busy trying to accept what he was that there was no room for any woman in his life. There wasn't one deity alive who was relationship material.

Then there was the question of finding mates for them. Sure, we gods were powerful and incredibly good-looking, but we were also dysfunctional and highly unevolved from an emotional standpoint. We were like children. With superpowers! Who would want to date any of us?

Narmer wanted to date you.

Narmer is an ass.

Agreed.

Then there was the whole picky thing. I mean, that there'd actually be someone out there my brethren would feel was their equal? Not gonna happen. The list of reasons as for the ridiculousness of this idea went on and on and on.

"Can't we just get everyone puppies?" I suggested. "We can make them immortal."

Other-me rolled her eyes. "They don't need puppies. They need passion! They need romance! They need a reason to live. Besides, nothing is impossible. Especially for you. Or us. Whatever. *We* are the only ones who have mastered our gifts. *We* are the Goddess of the Underworld, Pain, Chicken Noodle Soup, Campfire Stories, Shopping, Rainbows, Bad Humor, *and* Deception, just to name a few."

"You forgot Bringer of the Apocalypse," I said dryly.

"Exactly! We completely rock. They should name an entire species after us. Penguins! Yes. They should rename them Cimguins!"

What happened to future me? I'm so...crazy.

"You will simply need to use your powers," she said, "and choose the best match you can. Mold the situation to force our brethren to open their hearts."

This plan was beyond any degree of insanity I'd ever witnessed. But as I mulled it over, I could not deny its logic and the facts before me.

"Where do I start?" I sighed.

"What were you about to do next?" the Other-me asked.

"Kill Narmer along with his five brothers and sisters."

"Then you shall help them live," she said. "And you shall start the search for soul mates."

"Yippee." *Good times. Good fucking times.*

PART TWO—CIMIL AND RRROBERTO
THE NOT-SO-EARLY YEARS

Chapter Seven

Fast-forward through mountains of boring crap to Barcelona, Spain, May 1, 1712
(Hint: This is right before a certain vampire has his date with destiny. Poor guy ends up accidentally married. Oops!)

"I'm not going to sleep with Narmer's evil brother." I dealt another card from the top of the deck and slid it across the long, formal dining room table.

"What? I think vampires in tights look hot." Other-me picked up the card and frowned. "Reminds me of chorizo. And who can resist meat in an intestinal casing?"

Ick. "I can. You do know you're not inspiring me to continue saving the world, don't you?"

She began nibbling her thumb. That meant she had nothing in her hand. Gods, I was such a bad poker player. Pretty surprising given that was the only thing my flock, aka "the dead," did all day.

"Exactly why am I failing to inspire you?" she mumbled, adjusting the strap of her ballerina tutu.

"Because you're fucking crazy. Not much to look forward to." Sometimes, she'd wake me up, screaming I was on fire. Other days, she'd break out in hysterical laughter watching imaginary reruns of a show called the *Love Boat*.

"Crazy? Moi?" She reordered her cards. "Dammit. I got nothing. Fold." She threw the cards on the table. "Yes. I suppose I am. But I think your crazy boat to Crazytown also sailed oodles of centuries ago."

Perhaps it was true. I'd only become more and more disconnected from reality as time moved on. Reality was, after all, constantly changing.

"I have a good excuse," I said. "Look who I spend time with."

"Yourself," she said dryly. "You spend time with *yourself*. Speaking of, shouldn't you be packing? We have mates to find, and your work here is almost complete."

"We just got to Spain." I groaned. I'd spent almost four millennia doing nothing but causing mayhem, instigating mischief, destroying people's lives—all in the name of saving humanity, of course. Bottom line, no matter how hard I worked, Other-me still showed up for work every day to remind me I hadn't changed the future. I was beginning to think I never would.

"I've decided I'm not moving from this town house until we get another sign from the Universe."

"With whom do you converse?" said a deep voice from behind.

I twisted my body in the chair.

Narmer stood in the corner, wearing black leather pants and a white shirt with puffy sleeves. "You dirty son of a—get out!" Dammit, I'd paid my dues to this chaotic scheme. I'd let him, his brothers, and sisters live. Vampires, as they eventually named their species, were rampant in the world, in particular the Obscuros, who were quite evil and intent on enslaving mankind. All thanks to wonderful me.

Narmer held out his hands. "Wait. I only ask that you listen," he said, dipping his chin to stare directly into my eyes. Gods, his dark eyes still affected me. I wanted to pluck them from his head.

"Don't kill him, Cimil," Other-me said. Of course, Narmer couldn't see or hear her.

"Shut your piehole," I told her.

Narmer cocked a brow. "I am not familiar with the term *piehole*."

"I'm not speaking to you, unicorn slayer!" I spat and then turned toward Other-me. "Not a peep from you. Got it? Not a peep. I don't care if we all die."

Other-me shrugged and then mimed the "zippy lip, throw away the key" thing.

I took a deep breath and turned my attention back to Narmer. "What are you doing here?"

He lifted his chin. "I am here to apologize."

I bust out laughing. Ironically, so did Other-me. At least we were consistent.

I slapped my knee. "Funny, big boy, but I think

that camel left the sand dune four-point-seven millennia ago when you killed my Minky and decapitated me."

His eyes were hard and cold. "I behaved deplorably. There is no excuse." Chin still held high, he lowered himself to his knees. "I've spent thousands of years searching for the answers—what I am, how I was truly created, why no matter how many women I sleep with or drink from, I feel emptier by the day."

"Excellent! Then my wish to see you suffer for eternity was granted. It's about fucking time the Universe gave me something."

"I know you despise me," he said. "But let me assure you, the feeling is mutual."

"Then why the hell are you here, on your knees, asking for forgiveness?" I seethed.

He cleared his throat. "As much as my stomach churns with revulsion at the notion, I believe that…perhaps…"

"*What,* you filthy, fangy pharaoh?"

"Perhaps I have never truly gotten over you." He swallowed. "I ask that you give me thirty days to discover the truth, and if I am correct, to help me find a way to break this curse."

What a complete jackass! This monster destroyed my heart and wanted me to help him figure out if he still loved me so that if he did, I could help him to stop loving me?

Finally, someone crazier than me!

"The only thing you will get from me is the final blow. And I don't mean the sexy kind. Get up," I growled.

He was up on his feet, standing over me within the blink of an eye.

"You're wasting your precious time, Narmer. I wouldn't cross the street to poke you in the eye. And trust me, I really enjoy poking people in the eye."

"You must reconsider, Cimil. Do you have any idea the hell I have endured these past millennia? I go to sleep thinking about the woman I hate, who destroyed my life. I wake up with an enormous erection, still thinking about you. It makes me sick."

"Awww. How sweet. He likes you, Cimil," said Other-me.

"Shut up," I replied to her.

"Who are you speaking to?" Narmer asked, glancing between the corner of the room and me.

"Silence!" I barked.

Narmer studied me with curiosity as I completed my conversation. With myself. *Ugh. I* am *so crazy!*

"Silence is unknown to me," Other-me said. "But before you respond with one of your whimsical replies, like 'Shut your big whorey mouth,' I ask you to think before you respond to this vampire. What does your instinct tell you to do?" Other-me asked.

"You know exactly what it's saying."

"Then you must do the opposite," she counseled. "You must help him."

"No!"

"Just try it," she argued. "See what happens. Maybe I'll disappear!"

I clamped my eyes shut. *Shit, shit, shit. So unfair!* I clenched my fists and pasted on an expression that wasn't quite a smile, but was, at the very least, nontoxic.

"I hate you," I told her.

Narmer crossed his arms over his chest, glaring. "So this is your answer. This is how you choose to treat me?"

Wh-wh-what? Oh my gods! How dare he—

"I figured you might play your hand in such a way," he said and then bowed his head. "Very well. I came prepared."

I growled. He was making this "sucking it up for the sake of humanity" thing almost impossible.

"You *will* help me or—"

"Or what?" I hissed. I simply couldn't hold my tongue. "Or you'll screw some poor woman in front of me while draining the life from her, murder my beloved pet, and then remove my head? Again!" I pushed him, but he didn't budge. "Well, screw you and the leather pants you rode in on, because there is no one, and I mean no one in this world that I'd rather—"

I was about to say "kill," but Other-me interrupted. "Watch yourself, Cimil. Remember our mission. Humanity depends on you."

Dammit! Dammit! Dammit! I stomped my foot. This situation sucked camel humps.

I took a deep breath.

"In exchange for your consideration," he said. "I will return your beast. I merely ask thirty days to prove to myself you are not the love of my existence."

I covered my mouth with my hand. "Minky is alive?"

He nodded. "Do we have a deal?"

"You lied to me?" I growled.

"Yes or no?" he said sharply. "Decide."

All this time, I'd been without her, thinking my beloved pet was dead? And he said nothing? He let me suffer? *I am going to kill him.*

I pasted on a smile. "Yes. Yes, we do."

Narmer bowed his head. "I will return tomorrow evening at sundown."

He swooped from the room in a blur.

I grumbled several ugly words in the direction he'd left.

"You know, Cimi," said Other-me, "simply because you're supposed to help the man doesn't mean you can't play with him a little. I mean, I can't see how a little payback is going to throw us off track."

I planned to do a lot more than deliver a little payback.

In preparation for Narmer's arrival, I bathed in rose-scented soap, put on the lowest cut dress I could find—the red silk number with white lace trim—and wore my flaming-red hair in loose, wild ribbons down my back. My look screamed "sex kitten," though that term didn't exist yet, so I supposed the appropriate term should've been "whore."

I had to admit I felt excited dressing for him, knowing that I would see him and finally have the chance to give him a little taste of revenge. Because while the last four-thousand-something years had zoomed by, there wasn't a day that went by since we met where I didn't think of him. And trust me, I tried not to. I did everything within my power to drown the memories—knitting, gardening, poetry, hosting orgies—but nothing worked. Seeing Narmer again made me realize that it was because he and I had unfinished business. Mainly, I had a score to settle.

"Good evening, my goddess." Narmer appeared before me, grasping a handful of wildflowers. My first reaction was to rip them from his hand and beat him with them, but instead, I gracefully stood from my love seat, accepted them from his hand, and allowed him to bask in my hotness.

His dark eyes flickered with lust as he drank me in. "You look"—he reached for my free hand and kissed the top—"delectable."

I snapped my appendage away. "Thanks, but you can turn off the charm. I've been with enough of your kind to know how this vampire seduction works."

Narmer frowned. "What do you mean by 'been with'?"

I licked my lips. "Been. As in bedded. Played in the sack. Rode until cross-eyed. You do know that vampires and deities are sexually compatible, yes? Sadly, the rest of my kind feels they are too good to do the hokeypokey with a vampire. I, however, have taken a liking to it. In fact, it's like a competitive sport. I like to see which ones last the longest."

It was true. The touch of a deity wasn't fatal for a vampire, which made it ironic that my brethren saw nothing of value in their race, with the exception of Kinich, of course, who still held a certain morbid fascination with their kind. After the Narmer incident, I had a very long discussion with my brethren, keeping their origin secret to myself obviously. They saw the vampires as just another one of the Creator's creatures, brought into the world for the sole purpose of teaching us humility. A reminder of sorts to keep our egos in check. They were kinda, sorta right, but not quite.

In any case, while my brethren had a healthy fear of vampires, they mostly loathed them. I, on the other hand, viewed them as an invaluable asset to my all-out attempt to destroy humanity—er, save humanity. You get the picture.

Narmer raised a brow, and I immediately sensed his jealousy.

Good. The more suffering, the better!

"Well," he said calmly, "I suppose it would be

unrealistic to expect you to remain alone all these years. Especially given how beautiful you are."

Ugh. Did he think I'd be sitting by the phone—if we had phones—waiting for him to call? Idiot. "Let's cut the crap, Narmer. The deal was thirty days in exchange for Minky."

"Uh-uh-uha." He wagged his finger. "The agreement was you must allow me the opportunity to understand the nature of my feelings for you— thirty days to learn why I am obsessed with you."

"Which in your mind means…what?"

"We will make love. What else?"

"For thirty days?" I asked.

The man was off his immortal rocker. That said, this could be fun! "I will sleep with you one time, but only after you've satisfied my list of demands—"

"I said nothing about agreeing to a list."

"Do you want to play bowling for Cimi or not?"

He stared, calmly mulling it over. "I agree to nothing, except for bowling—my invention, by the way—but let me hear your list."

I snickered on the inside. "Nope. I will give you one task each day. If you complete the task success-fully, you may return the next day for another. At the end of the thirty days, if you cross the finish line, then the big trophy is yours."

He cocked one brow. "Mine." It wasn't a ques-tion.

I nodded. *Yeah. Like you're ever going to succeed.* "The whole enchilada, papi."

"Your words continue to perplex me. You do

mean sex. Yes?" he asked skeptically.

"Yeppers."

"I sense your trickery, Cimil. No doubt you will not play fair and ask me to do something I find morally repugnant or that will land me in hot water with others, your brethren in particular."

Hmmm...he's onto me. "I promise that I will ask you to do many morally reprehensible things; however, I promise to only involve the two individuals standing right here. Three if you count Other-me."

"Who is Other-me?" he asked.

"Don't ask," I replied. "The answer will only give you the uncontrollable urge to scream. Or send you into a crippling spiral of lusty fantasies involving twins. Redheaded twins. Point is, my terms are my terms. Take it or leave it." *Take it, take it, take it. I want to see you suffer...*

Apprehension flickered in his dark eyes.

"What? Aren't you a big bad Ancient One? Almost five thousand years old? What could I possibly dish that you cannot handle? Hmmm?"

He stared at me.

"Fine." I flicked my wrist. "You may leave, then. I have a date tonight anyway. I think you might know him, your brother Philippe." Philippe wasn't his real name, but many vampires found it easier to go unnoticed by humans if they attempted to fit in. They often changed names, moved to another continent, and tried to keep their look fresh. In any case, Philippe was about as fresh and big and bad as they came. He was also the brother who'd tried to overthrow Narmer and who would later end up the leader of the evil vampires, better known as Obscuros. Philippe and I were close buds now. It went against my better judgment, so that had to be a good thing, I supposed.

Narmer growled. "Very well. Name the first challenge."

I wanted to pull him in slowly. Make it easy at first. "I hate your name. It reminds me of painful memories. You will change it to…Barbara."

He tilted his head.

"Okay. Rrrroberto."

"Roberto?" he asked.

"No. I said Rrrroberto."

"Roberto. This is what I said."

"No, you have to rrrrroll the *R*," I said.

"Ah yes." He took a big breath. "Roooberto." He smiled proudly. "There, you see. And now that we have that out of the way." I blinked, and he had his thick arms wrapped around my body.

"Let me go!" I squirmed against his iron grip.

Damn, had he gotten stronger? Because I had the strength of twenty men. I knew this because I'd recently won a round of tug-of-war at the local watering hole. Got me a new horse and a few pounds of gold, including one man's tooth—he didn't think I would win. *Idiot. I always win!*

I wiggled a hand free and gave Narmer—errr, Roooberto—a hard slap.

His dark eyes narrowed, and he pressed his lips to mine. They were firm and masculine and sent shock waves of need through my system.

No! No! I would not let him do this. I fell for his alpha-male bull crap once, but never again.

I lifted my knee and landed it right on the mark.

Roberto doubled over, groaning and cupping himself. "Arrrrr. What the saints did you do that for?"

He can *roll his* R's!

I smiled. "That's what happens to little boys who take without asking."

"You kick little boys in their balls? You truly are evil," he grunted.

"Wh-wha—no! I do not hit children! Oh, shut up."

I grabbed him by the arm and shuffled him toward the door. "Out! Out, you crusty, old pharaoh."

I slammed the door behind him, knowing full well it would never deter him from returning, so I hoped he'd had enough for the evening. I sure as hell did.

I walked into my bedroom and pulled a mirror from the drawer to fix my makeup. I looked at my reflection and let out a slow breath. My pale face was flushed, my pupils dilated. Dammit. That man still had a grip over me.

"I don't care what the consequences are; I must destroy him."

Chapter Eight

The next evening, I made sure not to be at home, but in a place I knew Mr. Decapitator would easily find me. A place that would trigger a severe case of angst.

I watched Philippe, a lanky man with a straggly mop of black hair, pace across his lavishly furnished living room—velvety upholstery, gold inlay on all the wood, crystal chandelier. It was just as over the top as his clothing. He wore a burgundy tunic with blue piping on the sleeves along with white tights. Call me crazy, but I simply couldn't get into the men-in-leggings look. Not hot.

Philippe scratched his unshaven chin. "And you are certain, Cimil, that the vampire queen will not come after us?"

I laughed and then popped up from my seat. "First"—I held out one finger—"I have found her a distraction. A male who is, shall I say, perfect for her in every way." Yes, I believed I'd found her mate. How did I know? The dead of the future from the queen's very own dungeon spoke of a man that would drive her mad with lust. This man went by the name Andrus Gray. It took me a while, but I tracked him down and arranged the events, sending them on a collision course. Once he was in her life, the queen would think of nothing but him. Philippe would be free to start picking apart her army, recruiting the best for his own cause.

Why would I do such a horrible thing? Simple. It was a well-known fact that the queen was Narmer's right hand and the first human he'd ever made into a vampire. When he became tired of ruling, he'd made her the figurehead of his "good" vampire kingdom. Yes, I'd been keeping tabs on Narmer. Point was, however, I hated her. Loathed her. Which meant I had to help her find true love. As for Philippe—well, he was pure evil. A sick bastard with zero respect for human life who never got over the fact that his brother Narmer outranked him in this life or the past. That meant I had to help him.

See how horribly confusing everything was for me? Like equaled hate. Hate equaled BFF. Gray equaled pink. Good, bad. Bad, good.

One word: crazy.

"What about that fucking general Niccolo Di-Conti? He will never step aside quietly and allow us to ruin the army he has amassed."

I sighed. Why did everyone doubt me? "Now, now, Philippe. You just leave him to me." I patted him on the arm. "Mr. DiConti will be quite busy for the next three hundred years locked in my piggy bank." I flicked my wrist. "Now. Off you go! World destruction." I actually felt a little excited by how well my counterintuitive, evil plotting was heading for once that I couldn't help but do a little "Ode to Wonderful Me" clap. Next, I planned to hook the Obscuros up with Team Scab (aka the Maaskab, aka Mitnal's legacy of skanky priests). The challenge was getting two extremely untrustworthy factions to trust each other enough to work together. After all, that had been Mitnal's original plan. He'd simply failed to anticipate that Narmer would kill him instead of fight for him. *Idiot.*

Philippe dipped his head. "As usual, your abilities astound me. I am in your debt, Cimil," he said and then disappeared, sifting to his next appointment.

"Stop staring; you're ruining the moment." I turned around and saw Roberto standing in a dark corner of the room with a look of disgust.

"You're sleeping with my brother?" he barked.

"Well, yeah. How else would I get him to do my evil bidding?" I lied. "Or get him to tell me where you're staying so I could arrange to have your house filled with chickens while you slept?"

Roberto marched forward, seething. "You truly have no moral standards, do you?"

"Nope. By the way…what is that smell? Is that chicken poop?"

He smelled fine, but the look on his face was priceless. If only I could've been there to see his expression when he woke up to four hundred chickens using his house as their personal toilet.

He growled. "Very amusing, Cimil. But your childish pranks will not deter me."

Just wait until he finds out that I had his cistern filled with holy water.

"If I win this little challenge of yours," he continued, "you will never spread your legs for another man again."

How crude! And dammit! I really like it when he speaks dirty.

"Not sure I could give up Philippe," I said to fan the flames my little lie had created. "He's full of so many dirty tricks."

"Then I will have to kill him," Roberto said coldly.

Good idea. He's awful.

Wait. Where did he get off?

"Whoa there, RoboPharaoh. What's with plotting the death of my lovers? I agreed to sleep with you. Once! That was it. And you said you only want me so that you can learn how to break the 'curse.'"

"That is correct," he grumbled.

"So why are you acting like the jealous boy-friend?"

"I do not know! But you will not! Touch! Another!" he roared.

"Who do you think you are? You can't order me around!"

He pushed his tall body against mine. "I can do anything I like. I am the most powerful vampire in the world."

I stood on my tiptoes and met his glare. "The *stupidest* vampire in the world maybe!"

"Stupid?" His eyes turned into orbs of black, and when that happened to a vampire, it meant one of three things: they were angry, horny, or hungry.

Well, bring it on! 'Cause when I'm done with him, he's going to want his mummy!

"I've met dirt smarter than you," I seethed.

"Bitch."

"Asshole," I replied.

"God, you're sexy when you're angry."

"You read my mind," I growled.

Roberto slammed me into the wall with his body. Plaster rained down on us, and the room shook as his mouth connected with my lips, his tongue lashing and thrusting against mine, his hips eager and demanding as the rest of him.

"Dammit, woman, you make me so fucking crazy," he said in a deep, gravelly tone.

I tore at his shirt and dug my claws into his shoulders before raking them down his back. I wanted to scratch him and bite him and fuck him like a piece of meat.

"Aaah!" he bellowed as my nails left a trail of raw flesh.

"You like that, don't you." It wasn't a question.

He grabbed my hair in the back and pulled hard, forcing me to stare up at him. "Yes!" His delicious, angry lips slammed into mine.

My lips stung from the impact, and my body felt like it would burst into wild, magnificent, scorching flames of anger and lust. "I hate you."

"I hate you more." He released his grip and lifted me up. I wrapped my legs around his waist, allowing him to angle his hard shaft at the throbbing bundle between my legs.

He pressed himself into me, his pace aggressive and savage, while we mauled each other with our mouths. I'd never felt anything so insanely carnal. I couldn't stop my body from what it was doing— grabbing and touching and scratching him closer.

His hips moved in a frantic rhythm, my hips following in perfect synchronization, our bodies knowing exactly what to do, what the other wanted, and how to please the other down to the precise amount of pressure to apply. Yes, our minds were out of control, swimming in a sexual frenzy, feeding off each other's anger, but our bodies worked as one, sprinting toward that sweet, sweet finish line.

His hot, wet tongue slid down the side of my neck, and I felt the scrape of his teeth. "I want to bite you. I want to taste you."

He could have said he wanted to shave my head or wear my panties, and I would've agreed. The erotic tension was at its peak. Just a few more pushes and…"Anything, anything you want, just don't…"

He thrust forward one more time, and my body combusted with shock wave after shock wave of orgasmic pulses. I couldn't breathe or move a muscle. Tiny flickers of light danced across my vision, and my heart thumped wildly inside my chest. *Oh my gods, that was so magnificent.*

"I cannot resist. I must taste you," Roberto said. I suddenly felt the sharp prick of his fangs.

In that moment, my mind kicked in. *What am I doing?* "Get off me!" I pushed as hard as I could, releasing a burst of pain.

Roberto had not been expecting it because he flew across the room and landed with a hard thump against the opposite wall. Several paintings and a beveled mirror crashed to the floor. Oh, well, they were Philippe's.

Stunned, Roberto shook his head. "Why did you do that?"

"I was finished." I shrugged and smiled.

He sifted in front of me, clearly unhappy. "Well, I am not." He reached for the hem of my neckline, looking like he was about to tear my dress in two.

I held up my hand. "Back off, stalker. You haven't even made it halfway through the Cimi challenge. And a deal is a deal."

"But I—"

"Nope." I crossed my arms. "Touch me and the deal is off."

"You are evil and cruel." He scowled.

"Prrrreetty much." Gods, this was so much fun! I wanted to do a disco dance and chant that I'd gotten my fortune cookie and he hadn't. "But knowing you, you'll have a new woman in your bed before sundown. Oops. I forgot. You like them in threes. One to screw. One to kill. And one to drink from. Or is that two to kill and one to screw. So confusing."

Unchecked rage simmered in his eyes, but he managed to take a step back. "What is my challenge today?"

"Today…" *You've been extra naughty. What shall it be? What shall it be?* "You will tattoo my face on your back."

"Vampires cannot be tattooed. Our skin is far too tough for a needle to penetrate."

I flicked my wrist. "No one said my challenges would be easy. Off you go! And don't return until you've completed the task." I turned away, covering my mouth.

He growled. "Until tomorrow."

Gosh. This was getting super fun.

The next night, Roberto did not return for another task. Nor did he return the evening after. "I guess he gave up?" said Other-me.

I looked up from my book, *The Art of Whore*, written by that crazy vampire queen. She really made me feel better about myself.

"Pfff," I grumbled. "Not likely. He's a stubborn, arrogant fool."

"Cimiiil," Roberto growled from behind.

Right on cue! I looked at the grandfather clock in the corner. "A little late, aren't we?"

"I had to sift all the way to India to find a man they call the Needle."

The Needle? Hell, that sounded scary, even for me. I turned my back. "Good for you. But you've lost. The deal was one challenge every day. You've missed two days."

Roberto ripped off his white linen shirt and turned around. "Look at it. Do you have any idea how painful this was?"

I turned and gasped. "You have a full portrait of me on your back...riding on Minky?"

I. Love. It. It was the finest work of art I'd ever seen. And adding Minky was most certainly an extra-special touch.

"It's horrible," I spouted. "My nose looks funny." Again, I gave him my back and returned to my book, feigning disinterest.

Roberto made a weird little noise. I imagined it was the sound of a vampire about to detonate. "You said one challenge for each day. You never said I had to do them one at a time, one day at a time."

"True." I made a little shrug. This was far too fun to quit now. "I suppose you can have three challenges."

Roberto stood tall. "I am ready."

"Great. You will go out and buy me the finest villa Spain has to offer. Then you will go to the town square, proclaim your stupidity, and declare your undying love for me."

A flicker of a grin touched his lips, as if I were

ridiculous for believing these tasks would come close to challenging him. "Done."

"Dressed as a naked clown," I added.

His mini-grin melted away.

"And," I said, "after you've done that, you will donate all of your wealth to charity."

"What?" he barked. "Are you mad? Do you have any idea, woman, how much money I have accumulated over four thousand seven hundred years?"

I turned my head away, fighting a smile. Vampires were notorious hoarders of wealth—like me! Taking away their money was like removing a limb.

"You do not have to do any of these things," I pointed out. "You may quit at any time."

I heard the sound of his teeth grinding away inside his jaw. "I do not know the meaning of the word *quit.*"

"Sure. Just like you didn't *quit* us," I mumbled under my breath. "Ass."

"I did not *quit* us. You left!" he roared.

I popped up from the couch. "Left? Is that what you think, you moron? I didn't leave. I died! That little fucker Mitnal plucked out my heart and used it to save you! To make you!"

"You lie," he growled.

I stomped my foot. "Lie? I fought for twelve months to return to you. I was eaten by a shark! A fucking shark! Then I had to steal a fishing boat. Three times! Do you have any idea how hard it is to find fishing boats with a monkey's ass of a chance of crossing an ocean? Do you? Impossible! That's why they all sank! I had to swim the last thousand miles across the freezing Atlantic because *someone* had taken my Minky, and there was no other way. But I didn't care. I was worried sick that that bastard was doing something horrible to you!"

"Y-y-you didn't leave me?" he stuttered.

I gave him a push as bitter memories flooded my mind. "No!"

He stepped back with cold eyes. "I see."

"Do you? Do you *see, Roberto*?" I fumed. "Because if you did, you'd know that I would have faced banishment to save you."

Other-me tsked in the background.

Well, to hell with her! Err…me! Whatever. I was doing the best I could, but everyone had their breaking point.

He turned for the door and then paused. "I'm sorry," he whispered. "I didn't know. Mitnal said you'd left me, that you'd planned to have me turned into a monster all along. The gods' revenge for my arrogance. I killed him for saying that."

"Well, thank the Universe for small favors, but you're a fool to have believed I'd work with Mitnal."

"Am I? I know what you've been up to, Cimil. I know you taught Mitnal's disciples to use their dark gifts. You created the Maaskab. And the Obscuros." Yes. They were two of the world's most evil forces. The Maaskab, the twisted, powerful disciples of Mitnal and masters of dark energy. And the Obscuros, vampires who believed that innocent humans were their personal treats.

"So what if I did?" I walked over to the couch and sat with my back to him.

Just like all those millennia ago, he didn't trust me. But if he'd bother to see me for who I was, he would know that I was loyal and good-hearted. There was a method to my evil, mad ways. Those ways forced me to do things I felt were wrong. It was slowly driving me insane, tearing me up, piece by piece, leaving me with only my faith to lean on. Even that was on its very last legs.

"I know you are evil, Cimil. Why do you think I waited so long to see you? I did not want to face the possibility that my heart might belong to someone so horrible and cruel. Someone who only seeks to counter all that I fight for. However, my cold heart wants what it wants. I had no choice but to accept my feelings and try to understand them. But believe me, I do not want to love you. Not when I know what you are or that my love cannot change a being like you."

My head nearly swiveled off my neck. "This coming from the king of vampires? You think you're better than me? You've killed thousands of people, innocent people."

"In my early years, yes. I was reckless. But I have long since learned the error of my ways. I created the Pact to protect the innocent mortals from my kind. I created an army to fight my brother Philippe and the Obscuros. So *you* should not judge me, Cimil."

Well, la-di-da! Look, I'm a supercool Ancient One who can do nice things and isn't cursed with being the bringer of the apocalypse! "Well, maybe *you* should not judge me."

"How can I not?"

"If you bothered to look at what's inside you—a piece of my actual soul—you might find your answer."

Roberto left and a ton of emotional bricks came crashing down. Why did he have such a grip on me?

For the second time in my existence, I cried. And for the second time, Roberto was gone. I hoped for good.

Chapter Nine

The next day I packed my things from the town house. I would leave before sundown and try to finally move on with my life. Which, I realized, was something I hadn't done.

I know I mentioned this before, but time isn't the same for a deity as it is for a human. For us, a year feels like a second. A decade feels like a day—unless you're trapped by a tribe of randy midgets in the Amazon, hell-bent on keeping you as a love slave because they believe you're the Goddess of Eternal Pleasure. But I digress. Point is, although thousands of years had passed, my heart—the metaphorical one—hadn't healed.

But now it would. It had to. After all, I had love matches to make and a world to save. Neither of which were going so well. Other-me remained, which meant I was still dead in the future, which meant I hadn't accomplished squat. Probably because I wasn't making any progress with my brethren. Not one of them had fallen in love.

Take my brother K'ak, for example. Although he was the quiet sort, he radiated with an internal strength the ladies adored. They couldn't keep their hands off his long, flowing silver-streaked hair or that giant jade headdress he wore. So naturally, when I began my search for a mate, I looked for a woman who shared his love of jewels, knew how to wield a brush, and took comfort in silence. I visited every major city, every wealthy and powerful family, every brothel. I finally found the perfect woman for him, a gypsy with a full set of gold teeth. But sadly, she was human, so I planned to have her turned into a vampire once I confirmed K'ak's interest. After all, humans and deities weren't compatible physically. All went according to plan—K'ak was smitten; she was gaga over him—but the moment I had her vampirized, it fell apart. She became bitchy and demanding. K'ak dumped her after a week.

I tried the same experiment with Ah-Celiz, the God of Eclipses, and with Akna, the Goddess of Fertility; however, the results were the same. Once a human lost their humanity, my brethren lost interest. I seemed to be the only deity with a vampire fetish.

Well, as they say in Mexico, *"Menos burros, más elotes."* Less donkeys means more corn. Yes, yes. In this analogy, I'm the ass, and the vampires are the corn.

Anyhoo, I needed to find another solution.

With my footmen on my heels and bags loaded onto the carriage, I stepped out my front door onto the bustling street filled with afternoon shoppers, merchants, and the usual hodgepodge of soldiers and beggars. But the moment the foul stench of humanity filled my nostrils, something triggered me to stop. There was a subtle sweetness lingering in the air. The smell of…

"Minky?" I whipped my head from side to side. A gentle neigh to my right caught my attention. "Minky! It's you!" There, tied to a tree—of course, no one could see her but me—was my precious Minky. She was so beautiful. Gleaming white. Giant silver uni-horn. I darted over, but before I reached her, a man strolled by within an inch of the tree. She reached out with her soft little lips and chomped down on the base of his neck. Now, the moment she touched him, no one could see—thank the gods for that—but they sure as hell heard. The man screamed like a banshee.

"Minky! What are you doing?"

Unsure of what was happening or who was screaming, the people in the street scattered like chickens fleeing a fox. Except my footmen. They just stood there waiting. (I'd compelled them not to notice the bizarre and unusual, which surprisingly left them standing around quite often.) I tried to dislodge the man from Minky's death grip, but there was a loud crunch as she bit down hard and then it was too late. Minky let the man drop to the ground and licked her bloody lips.

"Minky! What have you done?"

She looked at me with her giant lavender eyes and made a little shrug.

I am going to kill that vampire!

I turned toward my footmen. "Take my things. We're not going anywhere."

It took a week, but Narmer did return. Of course, I knew he would. There's a little thing called stubbornness, and Narmer—errr—Roberto was the king.

Bastard pharaoh is going to pay for everything he's done.

I know you're thinking I still had the big picture to think about, but ironically, I'd landed exactly where I wanted to be. You see, killing him was what I wanted to do. But while that would have made me feel warm and fuzzy all over, it really wasn't a just punishment. Long story short, given the "do the opposite" thing mandated by my deceased self from the future, I would have to let him live. When I thought about it, there was no sweeter justice than letting him continue, trapped in his dreary, little life, wondering why after thousands of years he could not forget me. *Idiot.* He had my light. He'd never be able to forget me. In fact, I planned to give his obsession a little boost. I would show him a slice of heaven and then snatch it away.

"I know you're there, Narmer." He'd been watching me for the last hour as I finished up the last of my gardening.

I stood up and dusted the dirt from my hands and the front of my pink sundress.

"Roberto. My name is now Roberto. And if I

may ask," he said, "why are you collecting bugs?"

I looked down at the wooden bucket at my side. It was dark outside now, but I knew it was crawling with six-legged critters. "Interviewing witnesses."

One of my many wild gifts was the ability to transform humans into insects. I hated insects, all those little spindly, wiggly little legs. *Ick!* So once I cursed someone, they were tossed outside. Unfortunately, I'm not perfect. Once in a while, I lose my temper and transform someone I shouldn't. Then I've got to look for them and try to turn them back. It never works out well.

Poor, poor Smithy. But I'd warned him not to hurt Minky.

Yes, but it cannot be easy shoeing an invisible creature.

"Whatever you say." Roberto dipped his head.

I grabbed the bucket and turned for the house. "May I ask why you're here?"

He trailed behind me in complete ninja silence. "I have done as you requested."

I stopped and turned, remembering to stifle my urge to poke him in the eye. With a spork! "Excellent. However, you do realize that was one week ago—wait…" I plucked a strand of flaming-red hair from his collar. "What's this?"

"It is hair from the wig I wore. As I said, I did what you asked."

"You dressed like a clown in public, and I missed it? Hell, Narm—Roberto, where's the fun in that?"

"A naked clown. I wore only the wig. And your instructions did not include your having to be present. However, there are plenty of challenges left, so if you wish me to repeat the task, you merely need ask. Although…" He scratched his rough, sprouting beard. "You will need to loan me the money to acquire more makeup and another wig."

"You really gave up all of your money?"

He nodded.

I suddenly had the urge to spank him like a wild woman. With my tongue. While he moaned with excruciating pleasure that only I could deliver.

"You're serious?" I asked.

"Of course. I am a vampire. We are always serious."

Oh, that was rich. Or poor. Whichever. This ex-pharaoh probably hadn't gone one day in his entire life without a legion of servants and enough wealth to support a small kingdom. And he'd given it up for me? *Swoon. Sigh. And…melt.*

"What happened to the wig?" I asked.

"The crowd to which I declared my stupidity and love for you—which I would like to point out did not cast a very flattering light upon you—was more than happy to relieve themselves of their rotten vegetables while I stood there."

How had I missed this? *And…dammit all to hell! I'm starting to like him again.*

What? No! You hate him. He's a total cretin!

"Sounds like fun. So, why are you here again?"

Roberto followed me inside as I made my way through the kitchen, up the servant staircase and to my quarters on the third floor. "Pepe! Start me a bath, would ya?" I barked. Pepe was one of my hunky manservants.

Pepe appeared shirtless, rippling, shiny. I sighed with a deep appreciation.

"Yes, my goddess?" he said, standing tall and firm, like a mighty man-oak.

Roberto growled. "Why is this man nude? And why have you told him what you are? I understood this to be a secret."

I tilted my head, ogling away at Pepe. "He's not nude. He's wearing hot pants. You like? I had them custom made. They're all the rage in the future. Mostly for women, but I'm egalitarian all the way. For example, during the day, I put Pepe in them to chop wood while I watch. Then I chop his wood." I sighed for effect. "So entertaining. Almost as fun as when I have him lie down nude while I butter him with coconut oil. It's called sunbathing." I looked Roberto over. "You should try it sometime. That pale, pasty vampire skin doesn't suit you at all." Roberto used to be one of the yummiest, golden-brown men I knew, like a roasted coffee bean. Now he was the color of lightly toasted bread.

"Sunbathing. Very amusing, Cimil."

I shrugged. "I have my moments."

"Send him away before I drink him."

"Roberto, are you jealous?"

Pepe was pretty yummy; however, he was human and, therefore, untouchable. Roberto seemed to have forgotten that.

"Yes. Now send him away so you and I may converse in private."

"Pepe, do as the pasty man asks and start my bath. I'll be there in a moment. And I want the special scrub down tonight. I'm feeling especially dirty." I winked.

Roberto growled.

"Okay. Speak." I walked into my bedchamber and started shedding my dirty clothes.

Roberto growled again, and then his eyes locked on me. "I…I…forgot what I was about to say."

I stood in my chemise, knowing full well it was as sheer as a layer of morning dew.

"You were about to tell me why you've returned when clearly you loathe me and my evil ways. By the way, I think you ought to do an evil self-check, 'cause brainwashing a unicorn definitely falls under the sinister category."

"Ah yes." He scratched his bristly chin. "I'd meant to explain that little detail. It seems that after many thousands of years in the daily company of my men, she now believes she is one of us. My sincerest apologies." He dipped his head. "Perhaps with time…"

Ugh! "Blah, blah, blah…why are you here?" I snapped.

He walked over to my bed and sank down, staring at the floor. "To say that I was wrong. I should not have been so quick to believe Mitnal. I realize now that being raised with siblings who looked only to destroy me has tainted my view of the world."

I stared at Roberto and tried to ignore any feelings of sympathy. He'd caused me thousands of years of pain.

"I'd say I accept your apology, but us evildoers don't know how."

He ignored the jab. "I also came to say that you were right. I feel there is goodness in you. But I do not understand why you are helping the Obscuros and Maaskab."

"Because the evil in me says I should punish you. What better way than to help your enemies?" It wasn't true, but I hoped the answer stung a little.

Anger flickered in his dark, desolate eyes. He moved with dizzying speed and grabbed me by the waist, holding my body firmly to him. I was about to tell him to back off, but that was when I felt it. His warmth. His hardness. That little spark deep inside my chest and lower, much, much lower. For as many vampires as I'd gone to bed with, trying to rid myself of any feelings I had for their king, not one held a match to the bonfire of raw, needy, emotions Narmer—err, Roberto—had sparked within me.

I so hated him for that!

"I know you are lying, Cimil. But I do not care.

I know the truth about you now—you're not evil—and I am relieved because I love you and there is no denying it. Not anymore." He dipped his head and kissed me deeply. His soft lips moved over mine, gently at first, then harder. His tongue slid into my mouth, and he tasted sweet like cinnamon and sugar. His masculine scent was even sweeter, as if time had only made him more potent and delicious like a fine wine.

With one hand planted firmly on my backside pulling me into the hardness jutting from his groin, he moved the other to cup my face. "You feel it, too. Don't you, Cimil?" he whispered in that deep, lusty tone.

"Uh. Yeah. How could I not feel a giant pyramid stabbing me in the stomach?" I looked into his eyes, and that was when I saw it again.

Crap! I scrambled away and held him back with one arm. This time I hadn't seen destruction in his eyes, I saw my life. I saw him. I saw our lights pulling toward each other on an unavoidable crash course, destined to become an inseparable life force. I felt our hearts beating to the same easy-listening love ballad compilation that would someday haunt every high school prom for an entire cheesy century.

He is my mate?

No. No. No. The one male in all the Universe born for me, with the ability to make or break me. *This guy?* Why hadn't I seen it before? But now it all made so much sense. The way I felt about him even before he became a vampire, the Universe speaking to me through him, and my inability to move on.

"This can't be happening." I covered my face with my hands.

"Do not push me away, Cimil. You and I have unfinished business, and you know as well as I that there will be no moving forward until things are settled. We are meant to be." He lowered his voice. "You are mine."

"Yours?" I asked.

"Yes. Mine."

There he was. That man. The fearless king who stood before an ocean of people, daring them to defy him. Oh, the confidence, the power, the light of raw conviction and sheer determination. It radiated from some place deep inside him. He was magnificent.

And I would crush him before I'd let him own me. I would not let the Universe dictate one more piece of my life. Yes, I'd let him have a taste of me, of heaven, and then I'd leave him.

I pasted on a smile. "Perhaps I feel something for you, but the apology is not enough. How do you propose to make amends?"

Roberto's lips formed an arrogant smile. "I merely ask you to give me the chance to redeem myself, to complete the thirty days."

"Okay." I headed for the bath but hit a hard wall of muscles before I reached the doorway. "No. No other male shall touch you. And we will spend the rest of the month at the estate I've purchased for you."

Oh. I'd forgotten about that. "Is it nice?"

He nodded. "I spent half my fortune on it before giving the rest to the local orphanage. They are now the wealthiest children on the planet."

Awww…that was so nice. I loved children. Especially when they were rich. And boogerless.

"So do we have an agreement?" he asked.

There were nineteen days left. "Yes. But I'm bringing Pepe."

"No. No males. I meant what I said, Cimil."

"So you're telling me that you will not touch another woman for nineteen days?"

Roberto's eyes narrowed. "You do realize I must feed, and I cannot take from you—you are not human."

Oh, I knew. "Yep. Deal or no deal?" I couldn't wait for television to be invented. Watching TV through the memories of the dead from the future was so lo-fi. It sucked.

Roberto winced. "I will not bed them, Cimil."

"Nope. Not good enough. You can drink from all the dudes you like, though."

He stared.

"Men. I mean men," I clarified.

His lips scrunched up into a sour little pucker. "I disdain the feeling of holding a man in my arms. Women are much nicer. Soft and curvy and luscious."

Idiot. "Not winning."

"My apologies. Of course I will make the sacrifice. I would do anything for you."

I felt sorta tingly with anticipation. I was so going to enjoy breaking his heart. Or maybe I wasn't. A part of me wanted him to triumph as much as I wanted to punish him. How could I want both?

Ummm...'cause you're Cimil?

Good point!

"All right," I agreed. "I will go and see this magical oasis you've acquired for me. But if I don't like it, you're taking back your money from those orphans and buying me another."

Roberto studied me for a moment. "You jest."

"Not really. Why? Is that wrong to take money from orphans?" His mouth twisted with disapproval. I made an awkward little chuckle. "Oh. I'm only...jesting away."

Damn. I really am evil.

Chapter Ten

The villa wasn't more than a few hours by horseback from Barcelona. Of course, we took Minky, so that was, like, a two-second hop. (Insert visual of a large, well-built, powerful vampire riding on a unicorn with me driving. Two words: Fun. Knee. As in, to slap.)

In any case, I had to admit, the ex-king had taste. Exquisite taste. Hundreds of acres of rolling hills, thousands of vines bursting with grapes, fountains, fruit trees, and a beautiful rose garden in the back. The gorgeous three-story house was like heaven on earth. He'd spared no expense.

"You did all this in a week?" I asked.

Roberto gloated. "If you are not pleased, I will gladly live here."

"You're trying to mooch off me already? I'm not going to be your sugar mama, you hobo."

Roberto tilted his head. "Your vocabulary has become most peculiar these past millennia."

"Tell me about it." It was impossible to maintain a time-period-appropriate vocabulary when I constantly listened to and conversed with dead from multiple "time zones." Luckily, I'd been able to give up grunting after most of the cavemen left the pool of souls. But the dead from the present and future? They were abundant.

I entered the foyer, and the vaulted ceiling with an enormous wrought-iron chandelier immediately caught my attention.

"Ah yes," he said. "I had that brought in from a small village in Northern Italy." He waved his hand in the air. "My army has been working around the clock for a week, sifting to the farthest reaches of the globe to find the perfect furnishings."

We walked up one side of the grand staircase and reached a landing that had been made into a large drawing room. A log gently crackled in the fireplace giving off a warm glow to the hand-carved furniture and rich silk tapestries. Giant vases in almost every corner held fresh-cut roses. It truly was a Spanish palace fit for a queen.

"Yeah. I guess it's okay," I said.

Roberto snickered. He knew he'd totally nailed it.

"Our bedchamber is this way." He gestured toward a long hallway with windows on one side and a series of arched doorways on the other.

I followed along. "*Our?* My, my. Aren't we a bit presumptuous, vampire?"

"Always. I am a vampire."

Excellent point.

When we reached the last door, he pushed it open and made a small bow.

The room, with its Spanish-style tiles and white plaster walls, was simple yet elegant. A set of French doors, situated next to the fireplace, led to a private terrace overlooking what I assumed was the vineyard. A large bed stood in the center of the room, surrounded by soft, rich velvety red curtains.

"To keep out the daylight," he said.

"Why would I need that? I like the light."

He swooped in front of me and locked his arms around my waist. "You may cease with the games, Cimil. I have met your challenge and pleased you."

"Maybe." I smiled coyly.

"I plan to continue the pleasing with the same amount of enthusiasm and vigor as we spend the next nineteen days in that bed, making love. I will please you in every way a man could possibly please a woman."

I tried to swallow, but a glob of lust was stuck halfway down my throat. I found myself really, really wanting him.

You need to punish him, punish him!

But despite that being my evil master plan, that was not what I wanted.

Okay, punish him with really awesome sex. For nineteen days. That will teach him to never hurt you again!

He pulled me closer, and I craned my neck up to see his face. "Yes. I've had many lovers, Cimil. I will not lie. This has allowed me to perfect the art of pleasuring a woman and to prepare myself for you..."

"I always believed that"—I cleared my throat, feeling his erection prodding my stomach—"practice makes perfect."

"Uh-uh-uh, Cimil," said Other-me. "He'll only break your heart. Remember what he did to us?"

Ugh! She's right! Why was I so easy? So spineless when it came to him?

"Cimiiiil?" she warned. "Are you listening?"

"Shut up! Okay? I know," I barked.

Roberto glanced sideways, perplexed. "I am confused."

"I'm not talking to you." I pushed away. "We can't have sex."

"Of course we can. I am a vampire. I am able to withstand your touch."

"No, I mean I don't want to."

He moved so quickly, I saw only a blur as scraps of fabric flew through the air. The next thing I knew, I was on my back on the bed, Roberto just as naked as I, lying with his jutting shaft nestled between my legs.

"The smell of your arousal," he said in a low, gravelly voice laden with sex, "and the heat between your thighs, both of which have been driving me mad these past hours, do not lie."

Dammit. Damned vampires with their sex-sniffing noses.

"Cimil! You can't do this!" Other-me warned. "This sort of indulgence is what got us into trouble in the first place."

I looked at her, then at Roberto. His strong jaw and thick, sensuous lips, his exotic eyes, and long black hair falling about his face gave him the appearance of a mysterious god from another time. He was beautiful. And my heart couldn't deny what it wanted: to be whole again. He carried a piece of my light, forever connecting us. Revenge just didn't sound enticing any more. But loving him did.

He slowly bent his head and kissed me with an unforgiving passion, a yearning that didn't require words. I knew exactly how he felt.

Our lips moved together, and I felt his hand move down my torso and cup my breast. He massaged it for a moment before sliding down and placing his hot mouth over my nipple. His other hand worked its way toward that magical little spot ready to explode with the slightest touch.

"Gods, Cimil, how you drive me mad with your body." He lapped and sucked on my nipple, allowing the sharp edges of his fangs to scrape forth a gasp while his other fingers lightly grazed the top of the throbbing bud between my legs. "Yes. I like it when you breathe like that."

Holy horny pharaohs. My entire body felt like it might shatter into a million particles of light if he didn't release the pent-up pressure.

I quickly rolled him over onto his back. I paused briefly and stared into his dark eyes.

"Cimil! Don't do it!" Other-me barked in the

background. "He broke our heart, and he'll do it again."

I looked at him and then at her. *Dammit.* She was right.

I swung my leg around and hopped off the bed. "No can do, big boy."

"What is the matter?" Roberto's voice hummed with frustration. "I know you want me. Your body does not lie."

"No, it doesn't. But my human body doesn't know any better," I said. He now sat on the edge of the bed, staring at me, and I truly wanted to return to him. "But my heart does. Just ask it. Part of it's sitting right there with you."

His shoulders rose and then sagged as his lungs released a heavy sigh. "I feel it. I feel it very well. It has been my constant companion, Cimil. All these years, not a moment passed when I did not wish to die because of the sadness living inside me—your sadness, your loneliness. And mine, I suppose. I tried to forget you and what I'd done. I knew it was unforgivable despite what I'd believed about that first year we were apart. But as many women as I took and drank from, none washed away the mark you left on my heart." His head fell. "I finally gave up trying. Though I feed from them, I have not been with another for a thousand years."

Roberto sifted in front of me and cupped my face. "I love you, Cimil. I know that you love me, too. Your light inside me glows when we are together. It does not lie."

Dammit. Shit. Hell! I did feel it. I wanted to give in to it, to be with him, to forgive him for everything. How had he done it? He'd accomplished the one thing I'd never thought possible and that I'd sworn to never do: love him again.

No. It didn't make an ounce of sense, other than when the Universe gets involved, everything you know to be true flies out the window. You cannot help but bow down to its will. No human, vampire, or deity can resist her.

"Don't, Cimil. Just...*don't*," Other-me pleaded. "You know this will end badly the moment he realizes what you truly are—the bringer of the apocalypse."

Hell in a tie-dyed fanny sack!

The entire situation felt ridiculous! I couldn't win. On the one hand, I was wired to unknowingly drive every situation toward catastrophe, which meant I always had to row my boat against the current. That also meant I had to sometimes do bad, bad things and simply have faith that good would come from it. Roberto would never accept that, especially not when circumstances led me to help someone like Philippe. Or those horrible Maaskab. On the other hand, I knew that loneliness would ultimately lead to our downfall. If the gods didn't find love, we'd all go crazy and destroy the planet anyway.

But if I chose Roberto, I'd only hurt him, betray

him. He was better off without me.

I. Was. Evil.

I gazed into his eyes and then stood on the tips of my toes, planting a gentle kiss on his lips, savoring the warmth of his muscular body against mine. "I cannot be with you."

"I understand, my love. You need to learn to trust me."

"Yes—wait. No." I sighed. "I mean we can never be together."

He stepped back. "You are serious. I-I feel it in your light."

"I am, Roberto. I am serious."

He looked at me with suspicion. "But I sense something else. It's...fear."

I walked over to the armoire and opened it up, finding several silk robes inside. I shrugged one on. "Just leave, Roberto. And don't look back."

"I cannot do that." I felt his hot breath on my neck.

Why was he making this so goddamned hard? *Why?*

"I will not. You do not command me," he said.

Stupid, arrogant pharaoh!

That was when I exploded. "Then I will kill you. Do you hear me? I will rip out your heart and eat it while you watch. I will dance on your sticky vampire ashes. Do you hear me?" I screamed. "Do you?"

The anger I felt was so dark and foreboding that

it left a charred taste in my mouth. But I wasn't angry at him, I was angry at her. The Universe.

Roberto's eyes reflected the deep gash I'd inflicted on his soul. "As you wish."

He disappeared out the doorway, that image of me smiling back. From his…back. So ironic.

I burst into tears. Uncontrollable laughter followed. My life had evolved into one giant farce. I could do no right. I would have no love.

I sank on the bed. "Why me?"

Other-me was quick to reply, "Good question. I wish I could remember how I specifically triggered the apocalypse. Maybe then, you could avoid doing that one particular thing."

"Does it really matter?" I asked. "I'd find some other way to carry out the destruction of the planet. If I was designed for that, then *that* is what I'll do. I am evil. I always have been, and I always will be."

Other-me shook her head. "No, Cimil. Our actions are evil, but we are not. That's why I came back to stop you. In my heart, I want what's right. It just so happens that what I think is right steers the events in the wrong direction."

It was true. My heart was good. I wanted to be happy. I wanted Roberto to be happy, which is why I had to let him…

"Oh my gods! That's it!" I jumped up and down and did a quick lightning finger. "In my heart, being with Roberto is the wrong thing to do. I will only hurt him! That means I should do the opposite. I should be with him and subject him to my awful, terrible ways."

"You truly are bat-shit crazy," Roberto's deep voice said from the doorway. He now wore a new pair of black leather pants and another white shirt.

I ran and hurtled myself at his large body and began kissing his lips. "Yes. Yes, I am. And I'm going to do everything in my power to make you the most miserable man on the planet, hopefully for eternity."

Roberto peeled me off him. "While I do not understand what has occurred in the last ten seconds to cause you to change your mind, for which I am eternally grateful, you are making no sense."

"I'm evil!"

Roberto tipped his head. "Not helping."

"Aside from being in charge of the underworld and many, many other things, I am the bringer of destruction. The apocalypse. I don't mean to be, but it seems that it's the Universe's little joke. Everything I do feels like the right thing, but really, it's wrong. Look what happened when I tried to save you! I created vampires!"

He cocked one chocolaty brow. "And this means what?"

"It means that if I want to be good, I have to be bad. Really, really bad. Most of the time. Unless doing something bad feels good, then I do something good."

His face crinkled into a perturbed little ball.

"And you came to this conclusion how?"

I pointed at Other-me and explained. Obviously he couldn't see her, but I think he believed me because he made a polite little dip with his head to greet her.

She wiggled her fingers back at him. "Howdy."

"If you are, in fact, correct," he said, "then why do you still see this other future version of yourself?" he asked. "Should she not be gone now that you've taken appropriate actions not to do good things?"

"Excellent point." This whole space-time continuum thing is all very confusing. Welcome to my kooky world! "Maybe there's one thing left for me to do?" I winked at him.

He smiled. "Exactly how bad did you say you must be?"

I blinked and found myself tightly wrapped in his arms. "Very, very, very bad. I'm thinking we might need to see a priest afterward and confess our sins. Or perhaps spank each other as punishment for our very naughty deeds."

"I would very, very much like that. The spanking part, I mean. I am not a fan of priests. They always want to show me their crucifixes or moisten me with their little birdbaths. Most peculiar."

I stared blankly and then shrugged. "Spanking it is!"

He pressed his thick, warm lips to mine and plunged his hot tongue into my mouth. I felt the particles of my immortal light begin to vibrate as if rejoicing. They were finally going to be reunited with the part of me that went missing so very long ago. Or, perhaps, that part of my light never truly belonged to me. I was just holding on to it until its rightful owner showed up.

He slid his warm hands inside my robe and pulled it down off my shoulders, letting gravity do the rest. Not once in my entire existence had I felt uncomfortable being nude. The gods know I spent half of my life wearing nothing but a fig leaf. On my head. But standing before Roberto now, I felt naked for the first time. There were no walls of deceit to hide behind, no ulterior motives, no political agendas.

There was simply us.

As his mouth worked over mine at a sensual, expert pace, he gently cupped my breasts, caressing the soft curves with his palms and stroking my hard nipples with his thumbs.

He deepened the kiss, and his hands floated down to the curves of my waist. He pulled me into him with such force that the air whooshed from my lungs.

"Sorry, my love," he panted. "But I can't be gentle. I cannot be slow. I have waited far too long to be inside you."

Suddenly, I was back on the bed; Roberto stood before me and began stripping away his shirt.

"What? You're not going to just tear them off again?"

"My last shirt and pair of pants. And now that I am penniless, I will have to make them last." His dark, exotic eyes twinkled.

He was joking. If there was one thing vampires were good at, it was making money. He'd be back to his old, disgustingly wealthy self in no time.

He threw his shirt to the floor and shed his pants, standing before me tall, glorious, and sexy as he'd ever been. Thousands of years had not dulled his raw, male magnificence or my fascination with every hard inch of his body, especially his thick, long shaft. (Yes, this time I'm talking about his penis.) But what had changed were his eyes. Once they shimmered with a hunger for dominance and power, but now they glowed with something that radiated from deep within. A confidence, perhaps, that he always knew we were meant to be. Maybe it came from the satisfaction of feeling that we'd finally overcome our obstacles. Or perhaps it was the wisdom one only achieved through a lifetime of trial and error. I was sorry I'd missed that journey with him, because whatever he'd gone through had made him sexier than ever, a real man who'd replaced that enormous ego with something much more powerful. Love.

"You truly are a goddess, Cimil." He beamed down at my body.

And I am all yours. I opened my legs for him in a silent, blatant invitation. He didn't need any more encouragement than that.

His eyes flickered to black orbs, a sign that he was overcome with lust. Before I blinked, his hips were thrusting into me, his hard cock stroking my body into a tight, hot frenzy of delicious wave after wave of pleasure.

His eyes drilled into me, a steady rock among the whirlwind of euphoric sensations overpowering my body. "You feel so much better than I imagined. So hot and slick. But I need more." He placed his lips over the pulse on my neck and bit down hard.

I gasped at first, thinking that he was insane, that my light would cook him from the inside out. But as he vigorously sucked with his mouth and pumped with his cock, my human body was the only thing cooking. It felt as though he'd transformed my entire body into one enormous center of pleasure aching to be stroked by his powerful, hard body.

"Oh, gods! Oh, gods!" I couldn't stop what was coming. Feeling our pulses beat in synchronization to that erotic sucking and sinful thrusting, seeing his beautiful body—each muscle chiseled to perfection and covered with a sheen of sweat—his naked body flexing and straining to drive his thick shaft deeper and deeper, I couldn't hold back.

A violent orgasm ripped through my body. Roberto pushed forward one final time, releasing another avalanche of pleasure. He groaned like a savage beast as he poured himself into me.

Panting like he'd just sifted halfway across the

world and back again, he collapsed on top of me, nestling his face in the crook of my neck.

My mind spun in dizzying circles.

"Gods, Cimil, you taste delicious. Like nothing I've ever had. Rich and smoky and sweet."

I smiled. Maybe my darkness tasted like chocolate.

We turned our faces toward one another and gazed into each other's eyes. There it was again. The beginning, the end, light, darkness, happiness, destruction, the entire fate of the world balancing on the tip of a needle. He and I together. Him doing good. Me doing bad, ergo, good.

"Holy shit," I said, "we're the weights balancing the scale. Yin and yang."

He shrugged his brows suggestively. "My yin is wanting more of your yang."

I pulled my head back, wincing.

Roberto's dark eyes narrowed. "What now? Please don't tell me you have to go burn down a church or poke someone in the eye."

I shook my head. "No. I have that scheduled for seven a.m. tomorrow. But we need to talk—"

He kissed me hard and thrust himself into me. I gasped from the raw pleasure of his invasion. "There will be time for talking later." He thrust again and this time I saw stars.

∽ ∾

Five days later

Roberto and I made love twenty times in every room of the estate. I was extremely happy that my immortal body did not require sustenance and that his body thought of my blood as a giant energy bar. We banged our way through the night, rested during the day, and took long hot baths in between.

On that sixth evening, he stretched his long, hard, naked body across the bed and yawned as the sun retreated. I had been anxiously waiting for him to wake so that I could tell him a few minor details I'd realized over the past few days.

"Hi, sweetie," I said and kissed his full lips.

"Ummm. Good evening, my goddess." He rolled on top of me and instantly began to feed from my neck, groaning and, well, growing.

"Eh-hem," I said. "Honey?"

He grunted like a wild beast and started working his way between my thighs.

Hold those legs together, goddess. Do not give in. But he was much too strong and popped them open like a ripe tangerine.

Dammit. I would have to start working out my thighs. If only they had some sort of device for that? If I ever found one, I'd buy two. For every room of the house. Plus a few dozen backups. Because once Roberto got into position, I was completely useless.

I felt his moist head slide between my folds and tensed. The sucking and pumping, the kissing and stroking, panting and groaning would start and wouldn't stop until the sun once again set. I'd be lost to him. So very, very lost.

Come on, Cimil. Connect that brain of yours to those lips. "Roberto, honey," I panted. *Resist orgasm, resist orgasm, resist.* "There's something I should tell you."

He groaned, but did not release the powerful suction of his lips or slow the rhythm of his demanding body.

"Listen, Narmer—Roberto. I know that this doesn't seem important, but Other-me hasn't left yet. And, well, I think you should know that I don't think she ever will."

It was true. I'd seen her several times over the past few days. Each time, her clothing changed. More modern, more flashy. I came to the conclusion that she'd never leave. Whatever chain of events I'd triggered, my actions from here on out would only delay the end.

"I am confused by that statement, but make it fast." He panted into my neck.

"Well, you were right about me helping the Maaskab and your brother Philippe. And I will not be able to stop. I know how you feel about them."

He released a short breath and froze midpump. "I have vowed to wipe them both off the face of the earth. However, simply because you cannot do good, intentionally of course, doesn't mean that I cannot. I am not the bringer of death."

"So you won't mind?"

"Mind what?"

"Mind being stuck with me, even though I will be forced to sabotage everything you do?"

He smiled with affection and appreciation. "No, my love. I will not mind. As long as I have you." He covered my mouth with his and began that sensual rhythm, working his tongue, cock, hands, and body in one carefully coordinated dance to coax every ounce of pleasure from my mortal-like body.

I sighed with relief and relaxed into the sensual treat I knew my body craved.

"Just as long as you agree to marry me and have my children," he added in his low gravelly voice.

What? Is he insane? No. No way. I couldn't do that. Marriage was...was so permanent, and I was so young. A mere goddess of seventy. Thousand. Give or take a few centuries. And children? OMG. Why in the world would I agree to that?

"No." I pushed, and he landed on his back next to me.

He immediately sat up and glared down at me. "Why the hell not?"

"I would make a horrible mother. Can you imagine? I'd constantly have to do the opposite. Sure, baby, touch that fire! You want to play with that sharp knife? Okeydokey."

"Cimil, don't be silly. I do not believe for one moment that the Universe would want you to put an innocent child in jeopardy."

I snapped a judgmental look his way. "Really? But she'd be okay with ending the world? Babies and puppies included?"

He stared ahead, clearly pondering the question. "Perhaps you have a point; the Universe can be quite cruel, but we would find a way to make it work."

Knowing he wanted this so badly, I couldn't bear to look at him. "No. I can't. It's not right."

He lay next to me and tilted my face toward him. "Then, according to your rules, it is exactly what you should do, my love. You should have a life. A full life. With me."

I stood and shrugged on my robe. "I can't do it, Roberto. As much as I love you, I can't."

He was silent for several moments. "You are afraid. I feel it."

Yes. Yes, I was. "That's what I was trying to tell you. I have finally put all the pieces together. You, me, my visions…Other-me. Avoiding the apocalypse will never stop. We will forever be on the cusp, trying to prevent the tables from turning. One slipup"—I snapped my fingers—"and it all ends. We will never know peace."

"Then I will find a way to stack the cards squarely in our favor." He sifted from the bed and cradled my face in his large hands. "I will fix everything. Now, come back to bed, Cimil."

Always so confident, so arrogant. Did he really believe he could outsmart the Universe?

"We'll never win," I grumbled.

"I am a vampire. I always win. Please?" he asked with a deep, suggestive tone.

My eyes shifted toward the soft sheets, wrinkled from excessive bed play.

"Come now," he said sweetly. "We can worry about children and saving the world later."

"I am not having childr—"

He sifted me to the bed and left my robe in a shredded pile on the floor.

Sneaky pharaoh. "Okay, but can we play Tut-slut?"

He grinned. "I prefer bury the sarcophagus."

"Excellent choice, my pharaoh."

Epilogue

Fast-forward three hundred years past a bunch of really fun and exciting stuff to New Year's Eve 2012. Near Sedona, Arizona, the estate of Kinich Ahau, ex–God of the Sun. (Hint: This is right after a certain Sun God finds his surrogate. And right before a certain Goddess of Suicide finds her yummy Spaniard.)

"That was a dirty, dirty trick," I said to Roberto as he stuffed me into the back of the waiting town car outside my brother's estate.

He climbed in next to me. "Was it now?"

I crossed my arms. "Yes."

"Ah, but now, you've finally sworn to marry me and have children."

I had to admit, I was proud of my devious pharaoh. He knew how to play dirty. Yes, it had taken him three centuries, but he'd managed to outsmart me and back me into an impossible corner. I made the vow in order to save my brother.

"You almost killed Kinich," I protested.

His face gleamed with pride. "Your brother has always wanted to become a vampire. He will be fine. I left more than enough blood inside him, and now he has mine—the blood of the strongest, oldest vampire ever to live."

"And the sexiest. And most handsome," I admitted begrudgingly.

"True. So true. And the sexiest, most handsome vampire in the world cannot wait to bed you. I've missed you these past months." He grabbed my hand and began kissing his way up my arm.

"Roberto." I rolled my eyes. "We can't do this now. Everything is a mess."

He grinned with that arrogance I'd grown to love and fear. "You always say that, but everything always works out in the end."

I scratched my head. "No. It's different this time."

"You always say that, too." He leaned forward. "Drive on," he instructed the chauffeur.

Oh, but this time I really, really meant it. Something had gone very wrong. I'd taken a wrong step, done something I wasn't supposed to. I didn't know what, though.

"I want to marry you," he said. "I want a child. You said it might be possible with help from your sister Akna."

"Yes, but—"

"Cimil, you've had me chasing after you for three centuries, and now playtime is over."

"Maybe it is," I said coldly.

"Do not think to back out," he said. "A deal is a deal."

"I am not backing out. It's…"

Sadly, the news was bitter-bitter and the reason I'd been avoiding him for months.

"Tell him, Cimil. Tell him!" Other-me griped.

"What is it, my dove? Are you angry because I've trumped you again? I know my winning can become tiresome, but just as you are predisposed for destruction, I am predisposed for victory."

"No! You idiot!" I barked.

"What, then?" he asked.

"Tell him!" Other-me barked.

"I will. Just shut your clown hole!" I screamed toward the front seat.

Roberto's strong hand latched onto mine. "Cimil?"

Shit. Shit. Camel shit. "I had another vision. In less than eight months, the gods still turn on humanity." I sighed. "I'm sorry, my love. But we've failed. Somehow I've managed to bring destruction to the world anyway."

"But I thought you were making very nice progress with finding their mates. Kinich, Chaam, Votan, and, soon, Ixtab."

"I didn't move fast enough. That still leaves nine."

"Are you certain?" he asked.

I bobbed my head.

Roberto gazed straight ahead at the dark road. I could see from the way his jaw pulsed that some very serious plotting was happening. "Never fear, my dear goddess." He stroked the back of my head. "I will figure something out. I will save us."

"Why are you always so sure of yourself?" I asked.

"I managed to finally rid the planet of Philippe and the Obscuros while making a very deep dent in the Maaskab population. Why should I not be confident in my skills of undoing your treachery?"

Good point. He had done a magnificent job of playing his cards. He'd known that I had encouraged the Maaskab and the Obscuros to join forces recently—a truly evil union. Once the Maaskab had "vampirized" most of their population, Roberto hunted down Philippe. The moment his brother died, his bloodline went with him, including most of the O'Scabbies (aka the Obscuro Maaskab).

I bobbed my head. "It's not you that I'm worried about. It's the Universe." Everything I'd done—bad-good, good-bad—had been pointless. She still wanted blood.

"She is no match for me," he declared boldly.

"How sure are you exactly?"

He bowed his head. "Very. Otherwise, I would not say such a thing. I do not believe in fluffery."

"I want to believe you. I do. But this feels so much bigger than the two of us. Like that elephant with three heads we once saw at the circus." I sighed. That elephant was so magical. Reminded me of Minky, minus a head. "But your words can't change destiny."

He looked toward the dark road, thinking for a moment. "Very well. Then I shall use no words until I have delivered my promise. I shall not speak again until this is over."

Wow. He really was committed. Because a man keeping his mouth shut was like a fish not swimming. Or a sea turtle not reciting illicit, kinky poems about sparkly things. (Don't ask.)

"You would really do that?" I asked.

"I love you. And love is stronger than the Universe, than destiny, than anything," he whispered.

Gods, I hoped he was right. "I love you, too. Can we hit some garage sales in the morning? I need a little pick-me-up."

"But of course," he said. "After I take Minky for her morning ride."

AUTHOR'S NOTE

Hi, All!

Well, now you know how Roberto and Cimil fell in love. So. Crazy. Right? But now you're ready for the final installment of the Accidentally Yours Series, *ACCIDENTALLY…OVER?* (Book 5). AND! After you've finished that, if you're looking for more Cimil and her crazy gang, check out their NEW stories in the IMMORTAL MATCHMAKERS, INC. SERIES! (At the moment, I'm working on Book 4, *THE GODDESS OF FORGETFULNESS*.)

FREE BOOKMARKS:
As always, I have FREE signed bookmarks for my readers.
EMAIL me at: mimi@mimijean.net.
Please DO MENTION if you've posted a review so I can thank you and possibly throw in an extra-goody from my swag stash. (First come basis. International OK.)

WHERE TO HANG OUT WITH ME ON LINE?
Join my group on Facebook!
facebook.com/groups/MimiJeansJunkies/

Or, if you just want new release alerts, sign up for my sorta-kinda-monthly newsletter:

Sign up for Mimi's mailing list for giveaways and new release news!

Happy reading!
Hugs,
Mimi

THE IMMORTAL MATCHMAKERS

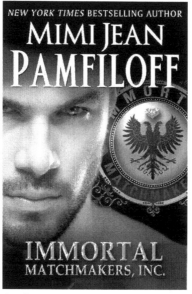

Because dysfunctional immortals need love, too.

SEVEN DAYS TO GO FROM LETHAL IMMORTAL ASSASSIN TO PRINCE CHARMING. DOES HE STAND A CHANCE?

Demigod Andrus Gray may look like every woman's dream, but when it comes to charm, he sees no point in pretending: He has none and makes no apologies for it. Behaving nicely hasn't made him the deadly assassin he is today. But is that really the reason he's still single?

The Goddess Cimil—owner of Immortal Matchmakers, Inc.—thinks yes. So when she foresees a mate in Andrus's near future, she's determined to make the match happen. That means hiring aspiring actress Sadie Townsend to help the barbarian "act" a little more civilized.

But are seven days really enough? And why does he suddenly have the urge to throw away an eternity of love for just one night with Sadie?

FOR MORE GO TO:
www.mimijean.net/immortal_matchmakers.html
Or keep reading for an excerpt!

Excerpt – The Immortal Matchmakers

CHAPTER ONE

"Godsdammit. I'm going to need a snack." Zac, God of Temptation and the most awesome mother-fucking badass deity on the planet, took his Bionic Man lunchbox from his black leather backpack, placed it on his desk, and went for his bologna sandwich.

"Fuck. Me. This can't be happening," he whispered and tore off a big bite while staring at the computer screen. *One hundred and fifty?* They hadn't even been open for a day.

His computer made that strange little swoosh sound, indicating more of this "email" crap was flowing into his "inbox."

He took another bite and nearly choked. "What the bloody hell?" Now two hundred and eighty immortals had filled out the online request form.

He looked over his shoulder, across the empty space of the twentieth floor, which they'd rented in downtown L.A. The big corner office remained empty.

Traitor.

It was well past noon, yet his crazy fucking red-headed mess of a sister Cimil, The Goddess of the Underworld, was nowhere to be found on their official first day of business. Of course, she'd insisted on getting the only office because she was "critical to mankind's survival."

What a bunch of deity-crap. As far as he was concerned, they were both equally valuable to humanity and both in this mess for two reasons: One, she was bat-shit crazy. And two, he'd trusted her. Having to open this matchmaking agency for immortals was all her goddamned fault.

That's right. My only crime was falling in love with my brother's woman. Yeah, so maybe he'd crossed a few lines, using his powers to try (and fail) to break them up. But banishment by the other gods to this hellhole of traffic, smog, and heat they called "Los Angeles"? Then having to come to this enormous, soul-sucking coffin of glass and steel— called an "office building"—every day to work like some lowly mortal slave to assist the unlaid immortal masses?

No fucking gracias, amigos.

His eyes darted around the empty space, taking note of its tragically undignified decorum of white walls, gray carpet, and artificial lighting. *Maybe I can spruce up the place with some paintings of naked women and chocolate—tempting shit like that.*

He shoved the rest of his sandwich into his mouth, dusted off his hands on his black leather pants, and went back to his computer, toggling through the profiles. *Vampire, vampire, demigod, my brother, my other brother, Uchben, immortal warrior…unicorn?*

"Hi. Are you Zac?" said a sweet, feminine voice.

He looked up and found a short woman with a long blonde ponytail and big blue eyes, standing in the doorway, looking very nervous. Her petite body, though covered in a horribly unrevealing dress with disgusting flowers all over it, was cute and curvy.

She batted her big blues in question.

He held up his index finger and swallowed down the lump of food. "Yeah, I'm Zac. Who the hell are you?" She appeared human, but this was a matchmaking agency for immortals only.

With an eager, friendly smile she approached, holding out her hand. "I'm Tula Jones. So nice to meet you."

He stood from his chair and watched her gaze follow his face up, up, up.

Her mouth fell open. "She wasn't lying; you really are big."

Of course. He was a deity—one of fourteen, over seventy thousand years old, and seven feet of masculine perfection right down to his godsdamned dingle berries. Not that he had any, because he was far too perfect for that shit.

Zac crossed his powerful arms over his magnificent chest. "Yes, I am big. In many, many ways." He cocked a suggestive brow, wondering how many seconds it would take her to reach out and touch him. The ladies always wanted a little feel. "So which lucky lady sent you?" It wasn't uncommon for the women to talk after an exquisite night with him. A god. A badass god. With a huge cock. And he'd been plowing a whole hell of a lot of mortal fields these past few weeks. Hell, what else was there to do? Cry over his broken, banished, badass heart? No fucking way.

"Uh, well," she said meekly, "your sister Cimil told me about you. Said I shouldn't be afraid or let you push me around."

Cimil sent me a woman to fuck? This Tula was a bit small for his taste, around five feet or so, but she looked like she might know her way around a cock. Maybe this day was looking up.

"She hired me to be your assistant," Tula added, her nervous eyes continuing to scale up and down his body.

Oh. So no afternoon booty delivery, huh? Maybe he'd go next door to the Starbucks and pick someone up. Banished and powerless or not, he was still a deity and completely irresistible to women. What his body didn't catch, his scent did. One whiff and the ladies swarmed like horny bees.

"And what makes my sister think I need an assistant?" he said skeptically.

"Your sister said, and I quote, 'He is a giant

asshat and completely useless, so he needs someone to do everything for him.'"

He wasn't an asshat. An asshole, maybe. But either way, was Cimil out of her immortal skull? Humans were on a need-to-know basis because they usually freaked the fuck out about the immortal community. They'd have everything from vampires to that nightmare of a head case, Cimil's unicorn, coming through on a daily basis.

Tula added, "She also mentioned that you might need some cheering up and moral support. And, wow, she was right about your hair."

"My hair?" He ran his hand over the length of his shaggy black mane.

"She said it screamed depression. Want me to book you a salon appointment?" Tula asked.

What? His hair did not scream "depression." It looked shiny and unkempt and screamed "badass!" The women constantly complimented him on how it set off his turquoise eyes.

Of course, they're usually looking at the bulge in my pants when they say it.

"I'm sorry," he said, growling, "but I think there's been a mistake. We're not hiring."

"Uh-huh," Tula said cheerily. "Should I sit here?" She walked around the desk and slid her petite frame past his body, sending a hard spike of arousal through his groin. She took the seat he'd just been in and looked up at him, smiling sassily.

"What are you doing?" he said.

"Your sister also explained that you'd try to run me off. Because, and I quote, 'He's a giant asshat and thinks he's too awesome to need help from anyone.'"

He growled and reached for her. "Okay, little girl, it's time for you—"

She leaned away from his hand. "Please don't kick me out. I really need this job."

He froze and then dropped his hand. *Gods-dammit.* "My sister told you to say that, didn't she?"

Tula shook her head. "No. But it's the truth. I need the money for college. I've only got one more year left, and my parents can't afford the tuition. This is the only job I've been able to find that comes close to paying the bills and is flexible enough for me to go to school."

Bloody fucking hell. She'd found his loophole. No, he didn't mean his asshole—his loophole. A deity's purpose was to help humans. It was hard-wired into their DNA from day one.

Now he had to help.

He scratched his unshaven jaw, unsure of what to do with her. Why would Cimil hire this naïve little human female to help them pay their penance—finding mates for one hundred immortals—or something like that? Honestly, the other garble the other gods had said at his sentencing about learning compassion and the true meaning of love had gone in one ear and out the other. The part about being stripped of his powers and banished, however? Well, that stuck like dog shit on a shoe.

"Fine," he grumbled. "You can stay. But just for the time being until you find another job."

"Thank you! Thank you," she said. "I promise you won't be disappointed. I'm a hard worker and great at organizing."

"Yes. Yes. You're welcome. You're welcome," he said blandly. Now where would he sit? He looked around the empty room that would also serve as their lobby. "I'll work in there." *Fuck Cimil.* She hadn't shown, so he'd take the big office. Let her sit on the floor. "Maybe you can start by ordering some…" He waved his hand in the air. "Some things to make this hellhole look less like a hellhole." Gods only knew how long he'd have to keep coming here; might as well make it worthy of a deity.

"Okay. I'll get right on it." She glanced down at the desk. "Is that a Bionic Man lunch pail?"

"Yes." *Silly mortal.* Could she not see the giant letters on the metal box, clearly stating "The Bionic Man"?

"My dad had one of those when he was little. A huge Bionic Man fan," she said.

Her father? But the woman at the very "cool and hip" store for younger humans had said that it was what the "edgy" and "fucking awesome" people used these days to transport their afternoon meals. No, he didn't have to eat but enjoyed doing it anyway. Yes, he was a stress eater. Okay? Even deities had their challenges. *Thankfully, I don't gain weight. I'm just a giant piece of awesome.*

Zac looked down at the lunch box and rubbed his jaw. "Well, it's a…a friend gave it to me as a joke." *Note to badass self: Must smite salesperson at trendy store for deceiving me.*

"Aww…well, I think it's cute," she said.

In that case, I will merely maim salesperson.

Tula scooted her body closer to the desk. "So, where would you like me to start after I order the furniture?" She flashed a smile that, despite its nervousness, was bright and cheery. Of course, that happy shit was completely lost on him.

"Ehhh…well, what exactly did my sister tell you?"

"Um, that you are the God of Temptation—now exiled and powerless—and she is the Goddess of the Underworld, also exiled, though she still communes with the dead. She is also a new mother to two boys and two girls, and, I quote, 'one dangerous mess of woman-hormones with giant cow udders.'"

"She told you what we are?" he asked. "And you're not afraid?"

She shook her head, her blonde ponytail flopping side to side. "No, sir. My momma raised me with an open mind, and I always suspected there was more to this world than what I saw with my eyes." She shrugged. "I love being right."

Funny. Me too!

"Ah, well. In that case, Tula, welcome to reality."

She leaned forward, lacing her hands together. "So is it true? You have an army of immortal warriors, kind of like the bad vampires in the *Twilight* book?"

He cringed. "We are gods. Fourteen of the most powerful creatures in existence, not…" He made a sour face. "Vampires." Of course, in general he didn't have anything against those sneaky sifting bastards. For example, his brother Kinich, ex-God of the Sun, was now a vampire, and even Cimil's mate, Roberto, was an Ancient One—the first of his kind. He was also once an Egyptian pharaoh, which made him an arrogant, ruthless fucker. Who could resist liking that?

He added, "We are divine, my dear human. Birthed from the Universe's womb."

She shrugged. "I still loved *Twilight*."

He gave her a look and was about to speak when he noticed something unexpected: Her aura.

Holy fuck. What. Is. That? In his seventy thousand years, he'd never seen a human with a purer soul. Not one. Looking at her was like gazing at a patch of newly fallen snow.

"You okay, Mr. Zac?" she asked.

He nodded dumbly.

"'Cause you look like you want to put whatever you just ate right back in the Bionic Man box." She scooted the lunch pail closer to him.

He shook his head. *So pure. So…wholesome. So…going to fucking kill Cimil!*

"Could you excuse me one moment?" He held up his finger, and she gave him a nod.

He marched into the empty office, dug out his cellphone, and dialed Cimil. As it rang, he closed the door.

"Hayyyyy looooow. This is Cimil. You've reached my voicemail because I'm busy licking Roberto's enormous sarcophagus or I'm allowing these tiny helpless degenerates to suckle from my ample teets or I'm plotting the destruction of mankind. Please leave a message and I will call you back as soon as never." *Beep.*

Zac growled into his phone before letting loose. "Cimil, I'm going to dismember you. First, you betray me. Then I'm banished. Now…*now* you hire a human who's, who's…" He couldn't say the words.

"Who's what?" said a voice from behind him.

Zac swiveled in his black leather biker boots to find Cimil. She wore a pair of pink lederhosen, gold platform shoes and her flaming red hair in an enormous bun on the top of her head. Her T-shirt read "God Milk?" and had two arrows, one pointing to each breast. Honestly, he still found it disturbing to think of Cimil as a mother. Worst of all, those babies had such an evil vibe. When he'd met them, he could've sworn he'd heard Satanic chanting coming from their cribs.

"Where the hell have you been?" he growled. "And what the hell do you think you're up to?"

Her turquoise eyes—the exact same color as his and the other deities—shifted around the room. "I am getting ready to serve my time for my crimes. Boy, we really need to get some color going in here. What do you think of a clown theme?"

He noticed Tula peeking behind Cimil.

"I'm talking about the human," he whispered.

"She is our employee," Cimil whispered back.

"Don't fuck with me. You're up to something."

"Why would I be up to something?"

"Because you're Cimil."

"Good point. But I assure you that Tula is our helper and nothing more. She's also taken, Zac, head over heels in love with a nice young human man named Gilbert whom she is to marry."

Oh great. Even worse. After all, he was the God of Temptation, and stripped powers or not, he was who he was. He liked tempting people. He liked it a whole hell of a lot. And Cimil had hired a human who'd be irresistible to him. He'd want to tempt her every which way possible.

"And," Cimil added, "because her heart is so pure, she's in no danger from you."

Zac lifted a brow, still not believing Cimil.

"Okay. So." Cimil clapped her hands together. "That was a tough workday. See you tomorrow!"

"You've been here all of two minutes, Cimil. And I don't know about you, but I want my punishment over as fast as possible." Living in the mortal world without any powers was already beginning to grind on him. How did his brethren who voluntarily spent their time in this world stand it? It felt like being confined in a small box. *I much prefer the freedom of our realm and being disembodied.*

Cimil tilted her head, studying him with curiosity.

"Why are you looking at me like that?" he asked.

She stared for another long moment and then her eyes widened in shock.

"Cimil?" He snapped his fingers, but she remained zoned out. *Oh great.* He hated when she did that because it usually indicated she was having a vision or an incoming message from the dead. Generally neither were good. "What, dammit?"

She blinked. "Woo! That was horrifying." She shook her head from side to side. "Zac, are you feeling a little agitated lately?"

"Your abilities to discern the obvious are impressive. What did you just see?"

"I'm not certain, but I sensed something is going to be wrong with you."

"Yes. And its name is Cimil. That's definitely it." And knowing he'd be stuck in the human world for a very, very long time while having to be around that little temptress Tula. How would he get anything done around here? He'd be obsessing over how to corrupt her. And help her, too, of course.

Because he was a god and needed to help humans. Yes, they were all quite fucked up.

Cimil puckered her bright red lips, looking genuinely concerned—a rarity. "I have a feeling that this sentence of ours is not going to be easy on you, dear Zac. So given the kind and generous sister I am, I'll hurry things along. Which makes it very convenient that I've identified the first client and laid out the entire game plan to avoid any hurdles, including recruiting—or blackmailing—same diff—our client's BFF. *Victimo numero uno* is as good as in the bag."

Okay. This was good. *Only ninety-nine more immortals to match up.*

She continued, "So I suggest to make things move faster, I focus on our first client while you work with Tula there to set up a mixer. We can throw a wild lovefest for all of the eligible immortals looking for love."

"Oh." Zac rubbed his chin. An immortal singles mixer would surely result in a shitload of matches. *It's fucking genius.* Not that he would admit that to Cimil. *But she does have her moments.*

"Now, get out," she said. "I don't want anyone in my office. Lots of confidential stuff lying around."

There was nothing but a cold computer and an empty desk.

"You're not getting this office," he said.

"Hey, it's the least you can offer after everything

I've done for you," she squabbled.

"You mean the fact that I'm being punished because you lied and manipulated me?" She'd promised everything would work out with his brother's woman if he followed her advice. Of course, Cimil claimed everything *had* worked out. Just not for him.

"Exactly." She shrugged happily. "And stop your whining. I got banished, too, and the only thing I did was tell a few lies, torture a few innocent souls, and save the world from ending. How fair is that?"

"Uh, because you were secretly driving the world to its end at the same time?" Of course, she couldn't really help it. Like him, she had her dark side, but ultimately served the greater good. Very twisted.

That Universe and her sense of humor. What a riot.

"Now shoo!" She swept her hands through the air. "Minky needs her rest."

Zac shook his head. Minky was Cimil's pet, a bloodthirsty and invisible unicorn. It was better not to speak of such things.

He followed Cimil out, and she closed the door behind her and locked it. "Okay. I have my womba class—boy, those four little monsters really stretched the old uterus right out—then Roberto and I have our daddy-vampire and mommy-goddess class. See you both tomorrow."

Zac was about to ask about the class, but then realized he didn't give a fuck.

"Tootles!" Cimil said, wiggling her pale gaunt fingers in the air. "And keep your paws off Tula! She's taken!"

Dammit, Cimil. She knew that saying that would make him want her more. He hoped she was joking about the taken part.

"Wait," he said. "You never told me who our first 'in the bag' client is."

She flashed a devilish grin over her shoulder. "The infamous Andrus Gray."

Oh, hell. That guy? Definitely not in the bag. "If that's the case, then we are going to need his best friend's help."

Glossary

Black Jade – Found only in a particular mine located in southern Mexico, this jade has very special supernatural properties, including the ability to absorb supernatural energy—in particular, god energy. When worn by humans, it is possible for them to have physical contact with a god. If injected, it can make a person addicted to doing bad things. If the jade is fueled with dark energy and then released, it can be used as a weapon. Chaam, personally, likes using it to polish his teeth.

The Book of the Oracle of Delphi – This mystical text from 1400 BC is said to have been created by one of the great oracles at Delphi and can tell the future. As the events in present time change the future, the book's pages magically rewrite themselves. The demigods use this book in Book 2 to figure out when and how to kill the Vampire Queen. Helena also reads it while they're captive, and learns she must sacrifice her mortality to save Niccolo.

Cenote – Limestone sinkholes connected to a subterranean water system. They are found in Central America and southern Mexico and were once believed by the Maya to be sacred portals to the afterlife. Such smart humans! They were right. Except, cenotes are actually portals to the realm of the gods.

(If you have never seen a cenote, do a quick search on the internet for "cenote photos," and you'll see how freaking cool they are!)

Demilords – (Spoiler alert for Book 2!) This is a group of immortal badass vampires who've been infused with the light of the gods. They are extremely difficult to kill and hate their jobs (killing Obscuros) almost as much as they hate the gods who control them.

Maaskab – Originally a cult of bloodthirsty Mayan priests who believed in the dark arts. It is rumored they are responsible for bringing down their entire civilization with their obsession for human sacrifices (mainly young female virgins). Once Chaam started making half-human children, he decided all firstborn males would make excellent Maaskab due to their proclivity for evil.

Mocos, Mobscuros, O'scabbies – Nicknames for when you join Maaskab with Obscuros to create a brand new malevolent treat.

Obscuros – Evil vampires who do not live by the Pact and who like to dine on innocent humans since they really do taste the best.

The Pact – An agreement between the gods and good vampires that dictates the dos and don'ts. There are many parts to it, but the most important rules are: Vampires are not allowed to snack on good people (called Forbiddens), they must keep their existence a secret, and they are responsible for keeping any rogue vampires in check.

Payal – Although the gods can take humans to their realm and make them immortal, Payals are the true genetic offspring of the gods but are born mortal, just like their human mothers. Only firstborn children inherit the gods' genes and manifest their traits. If the firstborn happens to be female, she is a Payal. If male, well…then you get something kind of yucky (see definition of Maaskab)!

Uchben – An ancient society of scholars and warriors who serve as the gods' eyes and ears in the human world. They also do the books and manage the gods' earthly assets.

Character Definitions

The Gods

Although every culture around the world has their own names and beliefs related to beings of worship, there are actually only fourteen gods. And since the gods are able to access the human world only through the portals called cenotes, located in the Yucatan, the Maya were big fans.

The gods often refer to each other as brother and sister, but the truth is they are just another species of the Creator.

1. Acan – God of Wine and Intoxication. Also known as Belch, Acan has been drunk for a few thousand years. He hopes to someday trade places with Votan because he's tired of his flabby muscles and beer belly.

2. Ah-Ciliz – God of Solar Eclipses. Called A.C. by his brethren, Ah-Ciliz is generally thought of as the party-pooper because of his dark attitude.

3. Akna – Goddess of Fertility. You either love her or you hate her.

4. Backlum Chaam – God of Male Virility. He's responsible for discovering black jade, figuring out how to procreate with humans, and kicking off the chain of events that will eventually lead to the Great War. Get your Funyuns and beer! This is gonna be good.

5. Camaxtli – Goddess of the Hunt. Also known as Fate, Camaxtli holds a special position among the gods, since no one dares challenge her. When Fate has spoken, that's the end of the conversation.

6. Colel Cab – Mistress of Bees. Because, really, where would we all be without the bees?

7. Goddess of Forgetfulness – Um…I forget her name. Sorry.

8. Ixtab – Goddess of Suicide. Ixtab is generally described as a loner. Could it be those dead critters she carries around? But don't judge her so hastily. You never know what truly lies behind that veil of black she wears.

9. K'ak – The history books remember him as K'ak Tiliw Chan Yopaat, ruler of Copán in the 700s AD. King K'ak (Don't you just love that name? Tee hee hee…) is one of Cimil's favorite brothers. We're not really sure what he does, but he can throw bolts of lightning.

10. Kinich Ahau – God of the Sun. Also known by many other names, depending on the culture,

Kinich likes to go by "Nick" these days. But don't let the modern name fool you. He's not so hot about the gods mingling with humans. Although…he's getting a little curious about what the fuss is all about. Can sleeping with a woman really be all that?

11. Votan – God of Death and War. Also known as Odin, Wotan, Wodan, God of Drums (he has no idea how the hell he got that title; he hates the drums), and God of Multiplication (okay, he is pretty darn good at math, so that one makes sense). These days, Votan goes by Guy Santiago (it's a long story—read Book 1), but despite his deadly tendencies, he's all heart. He's now engaged to Emma Keane.

12. Yum Cimil – Goddess of the Underworld, also known as Ah-Puch by the Maya, Mictlantecuhtli (try saying that one ten times) by the Aztecs, Grim Reaper by the Europeans, Hades by the Greeks…you get the picture! Despite what people say, Cimil is actually a female, adores a good bargain (especially garage sales), and the color pink. She's also bat-shit crazy.

13. Zac Cimi – Bacab of the North. What the heck is a Bacab? According to the gods' folklore, the Bacabs are the four eldest and most powerful of the gods. Zac, however, has yet to discover his true gifts, although he is physically the strongest. We *think* he may be the god of love.

14. ??? (I'm not telling.)

Not the Gods

Andrus – Ex-demilord (vampire who's been given the gods' light), now just a demigod after his maker, the vampire queen, died. According to Cimil, his son, who hasn't been born yet, is destined to marry Helena and Niccolo's daughter.

Anne – Not telling.

Brutus – One of Gabrán's elite Uchben warriors. He doesn't speak much, but that's because he and his team are telepathic. They are also immortal (a gift from the gods) and next in line to be Uchben chiefs.

Emma Keane – A reluctant Payal who can split a man right down the middle with her bare hands. She is engaged to Votan (aka Guy Santiago) and really wants to kick the snot out of Tommaso, the man who betrayed her.

Father Xavier – Once a priest at the Vatican, Xavier is now the Uchben's top scholar and historian. He has a thing for jogging suits, Tyra Banks, and Cimil.

Gabrán – One of the Uchben chiefs and a very close friend of the gods. The chiefs have been given the gods' light and are immortal—a perk of the job.

Gabriela – Emma Keane's grandmother and one of the original Payals. She now leads the Maaskab at the young age of eightysomething.

Helena Strauss – Once human, Helena is now a vampire and married to Niccolo DiConti. She has a half-vampire daughter, Matty, who is destined to marry Andrus's son, according to Cimil.

Jess – Not telling.

Julie Trudeau – Penelope's mother.

Niccolo Di Conti – Ex-general of the vampire queen's army. He is the interim vampire leader now that the queen is dead, because the army remained loyal to him. He is married to Helena Strauss and has a half-vampire daughter, Matty—a wedding gift from Cimil.

Nick – (From Book 1, not to be confused with Kinich). Also not telling.

Penelope Trudeau – The woman Cimil approaches to be her brother's surrogate.

Philippe – Roberto's brother. An Ancient One.

Reyna – The dead vampire queen.

Roberto (Narmer) – Originally an Egyptian pharaoh, Narmer was one of the six Ancient Ones—the very first vampires. He eventually changed his name to Roberto and moved to Spain—something to do with one of Cimil's little schemes. Rumor is, he wasn't too happy about it.

Sentin – One of Niccolo's loyal vampire soldiers. Viktor turned him into a vampire after finding him in a ditch during WWII.

Tommaso – Oh boy. Where to start. Once an Uchben, Tommaso's mind was poisoned with black jade. He tried to kill Emma. She's not happy about that.

Viktor – Niccolo's right hand and BFF. He's approximately one thousand years old and originally a Viking. He's big. He's blond. He's got the hots for some blonde woman he's dreamed of for the last five hundred years. He's also Helena's maker.

2018 RELEASES
THE GODDESS OF
FORGETFULNESS

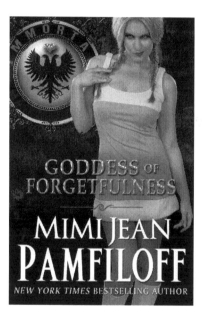

She's spent her whole life hoping to be remembered.
Until him…

www.mimijean.net/forgetty.html

SKINNY PANTS
BOOK 4, THE HAPPY PANTS
SERIES

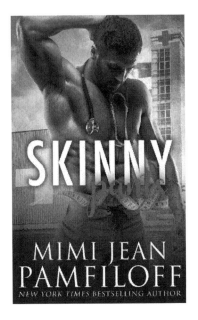

He's the doctor of her dreams.

She's got room to lose.

But this plump ER nurse will have to face facts:

A solid relationship begins when you're ready to take it all off.

www.mimijean.net/skinny-pants.html

DIGGING A HOLE

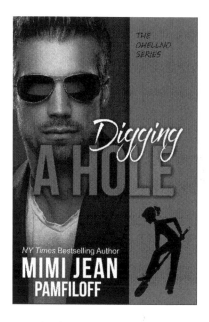

He's the meanest boss ever.
She's the sweet shy intern.
They're about to wreck each other crazy.

My name is Sydney Lucas. I am smart, deathly shy, and one hundred percent determined to make my own way in the world. Which is why I jumped at the chance to intern for Mr. Nick Brooks despite his reputation. After ten failed interviews at other companies, he was the only one offering. Plus, everyone says he knows his stuff, and surely a man as stunningly handsome as him can't be "the devil incarnate," right? Wrong.

Oh…that man. That freakin' man has got to go! I've been on the job one week, and he's insulted my mother, wardrobe shamed me, and managed to make me cry. Twice. Underneath that stone-cold, beautiful face is the evilest human being ever.

But I'm not going to quit. Oh no. For once in my life, I've got to make a stand. Only, every time I open my mouth, I can't quite seem to muster the courage. Perhaps my revenge needs to come in another form: destroying him quietly.

Because I've got a secret. I'm not really just an intern, and Sydney Lucas isn't my real name.

FOR EXTRAS, BUY LINKS, and MORE, GO TO:

www.mimijean.net/diggingahole.html

Spot the Phony Cimil Line— Answers

Which one of these lines was *not* said by Cimil?

1. "Welcome to my insane world. Please keep your hands inside the unicorn at all times."

2. "Berty, you think you're badass with that outfit? Your tiny manly parts will be on display when I dump you on the floor."

3. "Shit is my middle name. Except on Wednesdays when I speak Klingon, then it's Baktag."

4. "F***ing Cub Scouts. Give them some mistletoe and a few Christmas carols and they think they own the whole f***ing holiday!"

5. "Roberrrrrto, that man-skirt is not bringing sexy back."

6. "Okay, I am a good goddess. I am a kind goddess, oh, hell. No, I'm not."

7. "Oh! Pluck, Pluck, Eyeball is my favorite game! It's like Duck, Duck, Goose…but with eyeballs!"

8. "Helpful is my middle name—except on Saturdays. Then it's Jaaaasmine…"

9. "Roberto, baby, how many times do I have to tell you? You're MUCH bigger than my unicorn!"

10. "You may be the big-shot Pharaoh Narmer now, but you're still not wearing my pretty pink skirt to the pyramid celebration no matter how well it swirls when you shift."

11. "Hey, Roberto, baby, starting the goth craze early with all that eyeliner."

ABOUT THE AUTHOR

San Francisco native MIMI JEAN PAMFILOFF is a *New York Times* bestselling romance author. Although she obtained her MBA and worked for more than fifteen years in the corporate world, she believes that it's never too late to come out of the romance closet and follow your dream. Mimi now lives with her Latin lover hubby, two pirates-in-training (their boys), and the rat terrier duo, Snowflake and Mini Me, in Arizona. She hopes to make you laugh when you need it most and continues to pray daily that leather pants will make a big comeback for men.

Sign up for Mimi's mailing list for giveaways and new release news!

STALK MIMI:
www.mimijean.net
twitter.com/MimiJeanRomance
pinterest.com/mimijeanromance
instagram.com/mimijeanpamfiloff
facebook.com/MimiJeanPamfiloff

Made in the USA
Coppell, TX
11 November 2021

65586534R00109